D0610826

MODERN GREEK WRITERS

BETSY LOST

ALEXIS PANSELINOS

Betsy Lost

Translation
CAROLINE HARBOURI

KEDROS

The translation costs of this book have been covered
by the Greek Ministry of Culture

Typeset in Greece
by Photokyttaro Ltd.
14, Armodiou St., Athens 105 52
Tel. 32.44.111
and printed by
M. Monteverdis & P. Alexopoulos
Metamorphosis, Athens
For
Kedros Publishers, S.A.,
3, G. Gennadiou St., Athens 106 78,
Tel. 38.09.712 – Fax 38.31.981
June 1996

Title in Greek: I exafánisi tis Bétsy *(from the book* Istories me skilous)
Cover design by Dimitris Kalokyris

ISBN 960-04-1196-4

"DIG IT!" CRIED STELIOS LAMBRINOS and sat back in the chair behind his desk to hear the rest. In fact he didn't dig it as much as he pretended to. But Petros Kouvelas couldn't even breathe without boasting, let alone recount how he managed to silence his various opponents.

In the Piraeus office of the law firm Kouvelas, Restis and Lambrinos (three telephone lines and a telex address formed from the first syllables of their names with "Greece" added at the end)* the drawn curtains kept out the blinding sunlight; stirring in the tired summer wind, they threw glancing patches of light onto the cream coloured fitted carpet which were reflected onto the walls, while the glass on the framed renaissance maps in turn sent shafts of light to the ceiling. The bookcases – fake walnut – and the gold-embossed spines of the books within them added a formal touch to things.

The three friends had finished work quite early; they had closed the door between their office and the outer room in which their secretary Vipsy was also taking a break, flicking through a magazine.

* "Kourelia" in Greek means "rags".

Stelios Lambrinos was sitting at his desk with the other two in armchairs in front of it. He had tilted his chair back. His luxuriant moustache made him look a bit like a sea lion and his head was covered with a rich mane of hair. He wore thick-lensed glasses; behind the lenses his weak eyes wandered vaguely and ceaselessly, never resting for a minute on any one point, ever giving the impression that Lambrinos was in the grip of an enthusiasm which might only with difficulty be tamed.

Minas Restis listened to the story with a childlike smile – this very same smile had already secured them two important companies as clients as well as the services of Vipsy Comnenou who had previously worked for the law firm of Prokos and Stokos* on the floor above. Diplomatic relations with colleagues from this firm had, of course, been broken off; however, business had been going well for the three friends for some time, they had no need of anybody, and their pride in Vipsy was more than justified.

The oldest member of the firm was Petros Kouvelas who, according to the English system, worked least and earned most. He was of medium height with a slight tendency to plumpness, balding well before he reached forty; his face seemed sometimes that of a child and sometimes that of an old man; he had a high-pitched laugh and sole responsibility for preparing the bills that were sent out to clients.

Although it was fairly new in Piraeus, the law firm was steadily going from strength to strength. One success had followed another and their stock in the market-place had risen. Friends with most of the bankers and

* i.e. "Pricker and Sticker".

the banks' lawyers, friends with the agents, the shipowners, the freight agents, the insurance agents, the chandlers, the smugglers, the coastguards, the court clerks and the night watchmen, they now had two entries in the Yellow Pages – one in the yellow Greek section and one in the blue foreign language section. Their office had an air of comfort and wealth. It was cleaned once a week by the cleaning woman who did the stairs of the building.

Miss Vipsy took care to renew the flowers in the vases frequently. She was just twenty-two and had minimal previous work experience but had begun making love when she was fourteen. Although the consensus of opinion among her employers was that her typing skills were medium and her shorthand appalling, she showed an aptitude to learn and would soon become a first-rate secretary. In any case, they wouldn't part with her for anything: the girl had a perfect body, a pretty little face, and not one of the three partners had the slightest complaint about her willingness to make love during any of her working hours – indeed, she was often even ready to work overtime.

Her name, as she confessed to her employers under great duress one March afternoon, when they had tied her naked to the couch in the little room where the photocopier lived, she owed to a mad aunt of hers who had given her the name Vipsania (blessed martyr, feast day 3rd February) at her baptism. She herself hated the name, but everyone else, including her boyfriend Marcos, found it interesting and attractive.

"I told him," said Petros Kouvelas continuing with his story, "that the methodology of the reasoning was entirely erroneous and that the Court of Appeal had merely reproduced our own argument and judicial syllogism verbatim."

"Verbatim! Dig it!" said Lambrinos again, stubbing out his cigarette in the overflowing ashtray in front of him. His desk presented a spectacle quite unlike that of the other two: it was covered with a mass of papers all bestrewn with the ash that fell as he spoke, generally with his cigarette clamped in his mouth. The carpet behind his desk looked like a fairground shooting target. "And what did Garganourakis say?" asked Lambrinos, swallowing a yawn.

"'Friend, I got my little pay-off right here'," continued Petros, "'and as for the Court of Appeal, I shiiit on it' with that sing-song Cretan accent, you know."

"Justice!" snorted Minas Restis contemptuously.

"You're wrong, Minas," his elder said calmly. "It's a common mistake that everyone of your generation makes, not to be able to distinguish the grain of good in all this.... When you've learnt how to grease the palms of secretaries and counsel, then you will have grasped the essential meaning of Greekness, of light and kindness, the meaning of true democracy ... the rest to follow in the next instalment."

They all returned to their places. Stelios was reflecting that it was very selfish of Kouvelas to monopolize the girl during working hours – always during working hours – as if it were necessary for everyone to know what a fine and passionate lover he was. And in any case it looked a bit like common or garden sabotage: it always happened when Vipsy had work to type for the others, but never if there was work to be done on cases that Kouvelas handled personally. That morning he had taken her into the photocopier room twice, and they had been there for nearly an hour each time. Stelios and Minas, it seemed, did not have such violent outbursts of genital urgency – or if they did, they managed to wait until more suitable times.

Vipsy brought in three iced coffees and put them down on the smart little mats on each desk. Then, leaving the door between their room and the outer office ajar, she sat down to finish writing up the shorthand that Stelios had dictated in the morning. A pleasant little breeze from the open outer door of the office caressed her sweating skin under her light dress, cooling her. The murmur of the lawyers from their room as they planned their summer holidays, the midday heat which made the full day working hours so tiring, the unexpected second bout of intercourse that day and the eternal sanskrit of her own shorthand which she found so hard to decipher made her drowsy. She went on mechanically writing it out until five in the afternoon. In the evening she was going out with Marcos, so she absolutely had to get home early in order to shower and change. Her hopes to do a bit of overtime today with Minas would have to be abandoned.

She took the papers out of the typewriter, separated out the carbon copies, put them on Stelios's desk, tidied up her drawers and inspected her fingernails. She made one last appearance at the door of the office.

"Do you need anything else? Do you, Mr. Minas?" in an especially sweet voice.

"No, my girl," said Minas Restis paternally. "Only mind you don't forget the insurance stamps when you come tomorrow."

"I've got the forms and the money for them with me," she checked. To everyone, "Goodbye. Have a nice evening."

"Don't do anything I wouldn't do," said Stelios, having his little joke.

By late afternoon they were all ready to go home. Petros and Minas went downstairs first, leaving Stelios who always took longer to get ready. At once as they left the office a change came over them: their faces looked younger, their ties had been left on coathangers upstairs, their jackets too. Kouvelas set off towards his car, a white four-door sedan who answered to the name of Lulu. Restis had a helmet under his arm and walked to his motorcycle, a 400 c.c. Honda called Betsy who was chained to a lamppost. And while Kouvelas's car complained, considering that he had been kept waiting too long, Betsy welcomed Minas with the pertness that befitted her glossy red body:

"Hi, kid."

"Hi, doll," said Minas and he got astride her.

Stelios Lambrinos appeared last. He had become completely unrecognizable, since he now wore a long off-white cotton burnous, long-sleeved and with braid around the neck, leather sandals and a string of beads hanging over his hairy chest. In a bag slung over his shoulder were his cigarettes, Yellow Fellow (his cigarette lighter, which owed its name to one of those stories that we tell when we come back from our Easter holidays) and other necessities, such as the huge pair of moustaches which he only used in the office for professional reasons. This third member of the company drove a deux chevaux whom Minas and Petros condescendingly called "Marmaro".

At about the same moment the four exhausts (Betsy had two) spewed out their fumes and the three colleagues nodded to each other and set off towards their own destinations: Petros Kouvelas to Nea Kambara, Minas Restis to Hlapatsa Square, and Stelios Lambrinos to Batané.*

The capital was sinking into a light haze. Only a faint unseen breath of wind coming exhausted from the north offered some slight relief from the heat of the burning city.

WHEN MINAS DECIDED TO BREAK OFF THE SEASIDE ride that Betsy had begged for and to return home, the street lights had come on and were showing ever more clearly against the deep blue canvas that was unfurling down from the mountains. When he reached the square he made two tours round it, examining the café tables carefully, in case he should run into any of the other bike freaks of the area. Not seeing anyone, he turned into Kof-Mesik Street under the shady mulberries and stopped outside number 17. It was here that he lived. He attached Betsy to the trunk of a tree by her chain, shoved his keys into the pocket of his windcheater and, with his helmet under his arm, pushed open the door of the apartment block which was ajar. The single thought in his head was how to avoid the old people and perhaps also his uncle whose day it was to visit them. He needed to have a shower and to telephone Evanthitsa – tonight they were going to plan the summer holiday which, for the first time, they were going to spend together.

* Most of the place names in this story are fictitious; many of them are words taken from *kaliarda*, the Greek homosexual dialect.

The entrance to the block was illuminated by the red lights of the cars waiting at the traffic lights of the junction. The lift came down silently. It smelt of polished wood. The building was old, with high-ceilinged apartments, glass inner doors and decorative arches on the partitions between the outer lobby and the hall. His parents only used three of their six rooms; this apartment was the last remnant of the family's former prosperity; old man Restis had run through the rest. But the apartment had been saved. His mother fed her canaries and his father filed his archives wearing his dressing gown and slippers and an everlasting hairnet over his sparse straight hair, which always had a centre parting just as it had in the days when he first met his wife.

When his uncle, the general, came, his mother's brother, who had been retired from the army ten years ago under mysterious circumstances, a fourth room was opened up, the dining room at the front of the building. Old Mrs. Restis would order ready-made food from the "Hellenikon" – she had never been specially good at cooking and in any case the general's appetite would have exhausted a regiment of cooks. On other days his parents used to eat simple diet meals. Somehow, somewhere between the hallos and welcomes and the telephone call to order food, Minas would have to manage to escape.

The general was enthroned on the sofa next to old Mr. Restis, who had chosen to sit here so that he could go to sleep more easily when his wife's brother began telling his stories – the inevitable dessert that always followed their meals; the visitor had arthritis in his neck which made him unable to turn sideways and see Iolaos Restis dozing off. Minas's mother covered all the cages so that the birds would not be woken by the light.

His uncle greeted him as usual with a few sarcastic comments about lawyers.

"And what sort of clothes are these for a lawyer, Iolaos?" he asked in his loud voice, indicating Minas's motorcycle gear to old Mr. Restis. "You remind me of transvestites," he added to his nephew, "who go out at night dressed as women."

The old general's voice had a strong colouring in the upper octaves, like that of a hysterical old woman – this was something that he had acquired since retiring from the army, perhaps in an attempt to graft the tones of a denizen of good society onto the hoarseness of the barracks.

Minas gave his uncle a sideways look and greeted his parents with a weary smile.

"How is the pleading going? And the legal speeches?" the general insisted.

"How many times have we told you that Minas doesn't appear in court very often – most of his work is with shipping, Stefanos," grumbled his mother to her brother.

Explanations and counterexplanations were lost in a storm of coughing which the general used whenever he was cornered.

His aged linen clothes were yellowed from frequent ironing, yet they still bore the marks of a good tailor. Unlike other officers who always looked as if they were wearing borrowed clothes when in civilian dress, Uncle Stefanos was as elegant as an old dandy, although he deliberately dressed in a fashion belonging to a generation even older than his own. Standing, he appeared extremely tall. He stood almost a whole head taller than his nephew whose growth had stopped at just one metre eighty.

"Every profession has its own dignity, my young friend," he said somewhat didactically to Minas, "and its own uniform as well. What you're wearing now would be a lot more suitable for a student at a technical college.... Is that how you appear in front of your clients?"

"Why don't you leave us alone, you old stick!" muttered Minas, and, turning his back on his uncle who sat down on the sofa again with an air of wounded dignity, said to his mother who had not heard a word of his last response: "Mummy, I'm just going to have a bath and then I'm going out for the evening straight away."

Leaving the door open behind him he went to his room, while in his wake there was a surge of protests from Mrs. Restis and of grumbling from the other two about how young people can't be bothered to spend a moment with their elders – and about how very differently they themselves had been brought up. After putting clean clothes out on the chair in his room, Minas had a cold shower and soaped himself vigorously; this provoked in him an ever growing disturbance as it brought to his mind and to his tactile memory Evanthitsa's little ways.

Her pure, girlish beauty rose before him every time he saw his own body naked, every time he caressed himself with the soapy sponge; her starry, slightly myopic eyes with their pupils dilated like a baby's, her beautiful fingers with their well manicured nails, finely varnished; her childlike laugh, her easy good humour, her kind heart which could be hurt as easily as a child's knees.

They had talked of marriage; it was not a subject that

they avoided. He was not afraid of the idea, yet they were both wary of it. Like all young people, Minas believed in the depths of his soul that Evanthitsa was his great piece of good fortune, the amazing coincidence that you either meet or never meet in your lifetime.

And now they were going to go on holiday for a month, just the two of them.... And how her beauty excited him ... her sensuality so well hidden beneath the respectable appearance of a typical daughter of good family, until they were alone together in Kouvelas's bachelor flat. "I'll prickle her tickle," he thought as he used his palm to help the water wash off the soapsuds. "Telephone her! Now.... Quickly.... Her voice.... Her mouth!" He got out of the shower, towelled himself cursorily – for it was summer and you dried instantly.

The telephone was in the hall and was dangerously close to the dining room where by now the old people must be encamped. He'd call her from a kiosk as soon as he went out. He got ready, picked up his wallet and his cigarettes, took his helmet in his hand and came out of his room.

From the dining room came a dull sound. He half opened the door to the corridor, stealthily, and between the smoke which billowed thickly in the half-dark he could make out the battlefield. On the left side of the large dining table the enemy artillery thundered out one shot after another; the flashes came from somewhere near the vase of flowers and carried as far as the drawn curtains of the balcony door. The smoke was thick, covering everything. On the opposite side, in the trench, only a little bit above ground level – their feet lost in a time outside time – the general and his father, binoculars glued to their eyes, followed the attack of the infantry which poured out of the trenches onto the muddy plain, yelling battle cries. There was no longer any trace of boredom or old age on their faces, their movements were youthful and lively, their bodies quivered like thoroughbred racehorses waiting at the starting line impatient to surge forward. Behind the front, in the kitchen, his mother was unwrapping the packets of food that she had ordered from the "Hellenikon" and was arranging it in dishes, wiping her work-worn hands on her dirty apron; her heavy wooden clogs echoed on the tiled floor behind him even when he had silently closed the door and found himself alone in the dark corridor lit only by the red light of the lift.

On the pavement he stopped suddenly and his breath caught in his chest. Betsy was no longer in her place.

SQUEEZED INTO THE GENERAL'S ANCIENT CABRIOLET, Minas and his father scanned the traffic which was becoming denser and denser, immobilizing them.

"We took the wrong road to begin with," said Minas.

As the youngest, he was sitting in the back of the antique car, although he wanted to be in the front with the huge wooden steering wheel in his hands, kicking the pedals right down to the floor. But, as in a nightmare, he couldn't.

The two old men had leapt forward in response to life's trumpet blast: Iolaos Restis (who had never managed to understand how great his son's love for Betsy could be) considered the "motorbicycle" (which was what he called it, not motorcycle) to be a sort of extra powerful bicycle; and the general, still in full campaign uniform, had seated himself at the wheel. Instead of taking the Lykabettos ring road – the most natural escape route for thieves – they had succeeded in becoming bogged down in the traffic of Tzilve Avenue.

A wrenching pain as if his heart had been torn from his body kept Minas sitting between the two old men. His brain was working furiously in a sort of parallel hyperactivity far removed from the purpose of his thought ("Where could the thieves have taken her? In what direction? What harm might they have donc to her? Could they have smashed her dials or scratched her body?") and in his muddled mind, like a hopeless appeal, like a dirge, the lines:

"our two hearts will become great torches,
their dual light reflect
the twin mirrors of our minds"

kept repeating themselves.

"Stefanos, which direction are we going to go in?" old Mr. Restis asked the general.

My own neighbourhood ... it's a meeting place for bikers ... a magnet for thieves: Stelios's voice echoed suddenly in Minas's mind – words spoken casually in an unsuspecting past.

"To Batané!" he shouted as if with a sudden inspiration.

"To Batané? What an idea!" said the general with disgust and looked at his nephew suspiciously. "Where did you get that idea?"

"It's a well-known centre for bike freaks," Minas explained hurriedly. "And bike thieves hang out there too."

The two old men cackled with laughter. The words Minas had used seemed to amuse them no end.

"Turn here!" said Minas to the general. "You can get to the left."

"All right, boy, all right! This is a car, not a motorcycle...."

"A car – a car.... Forty years ago it was a bullock cart. Now it's a pram for taking babies out in.... Turn, goddamn you!..." He almost plunged from the back seat into the front seat between them.

Just then, an old woman wearing a kerchief on her head came up to the driver's window.

"Anything you can spare, may your dear departed ones be forgiven their sins.... I've got this little icon of St. Vipsania (blessed is her name) to keep you safe ... candles, incense...."

"Non merci, madame," said the general, looking straight in front of him.

"Chewing gum, peppermints," insisted the old woman.

"No."

"Herbs to restore your lost potence ... you know what I mean ... guaranteed, approved by the Ministry." Silence within the car. "If you look in Batané, you'll find what you're seeking," said the old woman, and her smile bared her toothless gums.

"Witch!" whispered Minas in spite of himself.

"Cross my palm with silver and I'll tell you who stole what you're searching for and who knows him well and can point him out to you!" said the old woman.

"Get the hell out of here, you old bitch," screamed the general and he thrust her away from the window with his hand.

The line of traffic ahead began to move again. The old woman continued to bob up and down between the cars like a fishing boat at anchor.

"Turn, go to Batané, General," said Minas. "Can't you hear what I say? The old witch said so. Turn!"

"Unlikely," muttered his uncle, turning the huge steering wheel, "Utterly unlikely...."

"Saint Vipsania, indeed," muttered Iolaos Restis, "that old woman was a fraud, Vipsania was simply beatified, not a saint!"

The Blessed Vipsy, thought Minas, and instantly Evanthitsa came into his mind, who would be waiting anxiously. Then, as if she too were a woman he loved, Betsy, with her glossy red body ... Betsy ... with the bright beloved curves of her belly, her narrow hips at the point where he sat astride her, gripping her between his knees, caressed so often with his hands, with his eyes such countless times.... Betsy with her shining chrome exhaust pipes that mirrored everything, her illuminated green dials measuring like the sighs of a lover the response of her whole being to his touch, to the curve of his wrist, to the pressure of his foot, to the way his back bent over her. There was no other woman like Betsy ... not one of them.

Batané Square was round, planted with mulberries. In the middle was a park and all around on the pavement were the tables of bars and cafés and spaghetterias. All round, at street corners and on the square itself, were scattered small groups of motorcycles, some chained, some supported on their stands, some lying on their sides. The general ordered old Mr. Restis to stay on guard in the car so that no one would steal it. A sardonic smile sketched itself on Minas's face but he said nothing.

By his uncle's side he passed through the groups of boys and girls arrayed like a guard of honour around the motorcycles; one by one he looked at the tails, the masks, the wheel rims – whatever might betray the presence of Betsy among them. There was nothing to be seen. The smell of pizza mingled with the smell of unburnt petrol from the exhaust pipes. What had they better do? The tour of the square hadn't resulted in anything. They stood undecided in the middle of it. The general, who had changed in the last hour, looked like someone who is attempting to pass unobserved, sometimes hunched up and sometimes trying to act naturally. Minas was ready to accept the vainness of the endeavour when all of a sudden a quiet hoarse voice stopped him in his tracks.

"Tell him to find Soulis."

He turned round to see who had spoken; but there was no one. They were standing beside a table which must just have been vacated; for a hastily and clumsily stubbed out cigarette, stained red on its white filter, was still smoking, and there were empty glasses still beaded with moisture from the chilled water they had contained, and a cup of coffee still steaming since only one or two hasty mouthfuls had been drunk. He heard the voice again and it was coming from the cup of coffee.

"Tell him to find Soulis. Soulis knows...."

Inanimate objects stand beside us and help us in our hour of need: the silent witnesses of reality. It was an unlooked for bit of help; Minas gazed at the coffee cup gratefully. "Thank you, kind coffee, thank you," he said, then to the general abruptly, "Find Soulis, you old stick." His mother's brother stared at him, thunderstruck, first as if he didn't understand, then as if the truth was being inescapably unveiled before his eyes. He bowed his head and smiled apologetically, casting a sideways look at his nephew.

"So you know it all, then," he said.

"Yes, everything," said Minas, who in fact knew quite a lot about his uncle but not everything.

"All of us have...." began the general.

"That's your business, General," Minas interrupted, "I don't want to know about your pale pink secrets but about my bright red motorcycle. And Soulis knows...."

"It's highly likely," murmured the old man to himself, broken, "it's highly likely. He's done it before countless times ... but to do it to your motorcycle!"

"Forward march! Don't waste time!" ordered Minas.

With the general in front, they crossed to the pavement opposite. A bar with a narrow doorway, red lights and a wooden partition along the wall, opposite the bar with its high stools. Outside on the pavement were only three tables, all of them empty; more than anything else, it had the feel of a club whose members had not turned up that evening. A barman of indeterminate age with a badly dyed wig and plump cheeks stood behind the bar.

"Good evening!" said the general formally in his usual voice.

"Good evening," replied the barman with a smile that had begun spreading over his face from the minute that he had seen them walk in but which now lost its way and took on an unsuitably official air.

"I'm looking for Soulis," said the general in a low voice.

The barman weighed up Minas, who was standing next to his uncle, with a calculating look, and then, as if he didn't quite understand,

"For a gang bang, would it be, General?" he asked rather insolently.[*] "Oh deary me, *what* a shame, Soulis has just left.... It *does* look as if he's given us the old heave-ho once and for all today."

"How come?" asked the general (in a voice just like his sister's, thought Minas).

"He's changing scene, he said. He said to tell you goodbye. He's sick of giving blow jobs and of being the one who gets fucked."

"That's a lie!" broke out the general. "Just listen here, Georgia," he said in a quieter voice and leaned threateningly towards the barman. "This kid here isn't a tart, he's my sister's son, not a rent boy. I want an explanation: we're trying to find the motorcycle which that little cock sucker's nicked.... So come on, where's he gone?"

There was a rapid exchange of glances. Minas understood that the barman with the wig and his uncle would like to be alone for a little while. It was an opportunity.

In the corner of the bar was a red pay phone. He put a coin in and dialled Evanthitsa's number. She answered immediately, as if she had been sitting right by the telephone – and of course she would have been waiting. Her voice was high pitched with impatience and anxiety. As calmly as he could, he explained to her what had happened. Their date would have to be put off till tomorrow, God willing. He had no idea what still lay ahead of him tonight.

Was Evanthitsa being understanding, or was she angry? He could never be sure – this was part of her charm for him. And for certain she had not understood

[*] In the original text the conversation between the general and the barman is in *kaliarda*, the Greek homosexual dialect.

what Betsy meant to him. Why had he not gone to the police straight away? Why was he getting involved in a search which would probably turn out to be fruitless and which wasn't without risk? As far as Evanthitsa was concerned, their meeting could have gone ahead without Betsy: they could have taken a taxi to go down to Piraeus where Kouvelas's flat was, then come back by train, walking to the station. But for Minas their meeting made no sense without Betsy – the whole raison d'être for going out seemed to have been lost: nothing else could ever give thc excitement of their ride on the bike.

The general's conversation with Georgia at the bar did not seem to have borne fruit. His uncle had the air of trying to weigh up and compare what he had just heard with what he knew himself, or with what people whom he trusted more than the barman had told him.

Georgia was looking suspiciously at the young lad: she hadn't believed a word that the general had said about sisters and nephews and what have you – she knew the old queen too well, and what she was capable of putting across in order to get what she wanted.

Minas's uncle pushed his nephew out of the bar without saying goodbye.

"We didn't learn anything worth knowing here," he said with a deep sigh, "let's go to Soulis's neighbourhood in case we come across anything there. Just bear in mind, though, that you mustn't ever breathe a word about all this to your parents.... That faggot was lying to me. I know where we'll be able to find out...."

They crossed the square again to get back to the car, passing a waiter carrying a tray loaded with dirty plates and glasses. Minas thought that among them he saw his friend.

"Thanks, kind coffee, thanks" he whispered.

"Who the hell does that lunatic think he's talking to?" said a half-finished ice-cream to the sugar pot beside it.

"DIG IT," SAID STELIOS LAMBRINOS and sat down on the paving stones in the courtyard under the vine. He was holding a can of coca-cola which he had just opened and, balancing it on the ground, he prepared to light his filterless cigarette with Yellow Fellow. "Dig it," he said again.

"Click!" said Yellow Fellow.

But Stelios did not get into conversation with him because he didn't believe that objects ... whatsitted ... you know.... He was not a dreamer like Restis – an animist, as Kouvelas would say. Stelios heard the click of his lighter and saw the flame which would light his cigarette. Of course, whenever Restis started on about that sort of thing, he would gaze at him and clap his hands like a baby and giggle enthusiastically, but his small eyes would be searching the other's face in case he was having him on, in case he should suddenly become serious again and leave Stelios out on a limb. Being made fun of by people was something that Stelios had always had a fear of, ever since he was a child. By himself, he could "defuse" more easily.

This was one of his own expressions, taken from friends who had learnt it and similar things while doing their military service. Stelios had had the luck to be exempted from military service because of his poor sight, but he had turned it into his own expression, had adopted it into his own personal vocabulary. "Defusing" meant letting go completely, throwing aside his tie, unsticking his moustache, in the summer even going barefoot; defusing, as in "we remove the fuse from the electrical panel and all the notice boards, the signs, the lights, the posturings go out and we can be at peace...." Stelios had learnt to play alone, to amuse himself alone, to talk alone – yes, even to talk to himself. He was used to it, in fact. Sometimes when he was absorbed in his work at the office he could be heard talking to himself out loud, to the great annoyance of Restis and Kouvelas, while Vipsy smothered her giggles with the palms of her hands (Vipsy in fact had palms on her feet too – this was a secret which Petros had discovered first and which the others had later verified for themselves). Lambrinos's habit of talking to himself was one of the many things which the other two partners did not approve of – Kouvelas, particularly, since he was concerned with achieving a perfect aristocratic tone for the office, but Minas too, who copied Petros in professional matters.

Anyway, having by now "defused", still wearing his burnous and his beads but minus moustache, he was sitting and enjoying a peaceful summer evening in the coolness of the courtyard of his family home. As the hours went by, his mind managed to push all memories of the office or of cases into the background; since he had not arranged to meet anyone tonight, didn't feel the need to arrange anything, he drifted among violet clouds like those which at sunset had appeared low on the horizon.

His parents were out. The house and the neighbourhood (quiet, without traffic, with low houses, little gardens and a defunct factory behind a high stone wall) was plunged into silence. Now and then from far off came the dull sound of the bus terminus at Batané, only to fade away quickly, whereupon the silence spread once more.

Marmaro was half asleep at the kerb outside the house. Stelios himself didn't call her Marmaro: Kouvelas and Restis gave her this name. Stelios did not call her anything – only occasionally he referred to her as "the washtub". Marmaro had never done anything to make her valuable enough in the eyes of her master for him to name her. Stelios did not have good relations with machines in general, or with anything that seemed complicated to him. Yellow Fellow, of course (who meanwhile had said "Click!" two more times) was something else; he had a history and had been blessed with a name – but not with conversation, however.

The lighter himself had a great sense of his own worth and his experience of life could not be compared with that of other lighters from the same batch. He had begun his career in the handbag of Penny Karakoulia, where he lived squeezed in with numerous bits and pieces, such as a spiral-bound notepad with nonsense written in teeny weeny letters by a pencil who also lived there, and a little mirror which advertised "Kithara" sewing thread to its fellow-inhabitants, paper handkerchiefs, Vicks for the nose, a fat leather wallet of indeterminate colour, a key ring with most ill-mannered keys, noisy and aggressive, who kept hitting everyone, a packet of contraceptives, another packet containing a black velvet ribbon on which was a small jewel which no one (except Yellow Fellow) knew what it was doing there, a hairbrush and comb who cohabited and coupled shamelessly in front of everyone, and some other things which he had now forgotten. Yellow Fellow rarely emerged from the bag, where his mistress had placed him not because she smoked herself but because her escorts smoked. The only thing about these men that he managed to get a glimpse of was their supernaturally huge noses and their eyes which squinted as they tried to see whether he (Yellow Fellow) would do his work well. And then wham! Back inside. Later, suddenly, he changed masters.

It was the day when he finally discovered what business the box with the velvet ribbon had with the rest of them. He had been put on the chest of drawers, lying on top of Lambrinos's cigarette packet and he realized that, when she was with Lambrinos, his mistress took off all her clothes and put the black ribbon round her neck. ("I long for it," commented Stelios in a loud voice.) He had been sure that he would have to pay for his indiscretion; and indeed from that day Yellow Fellow changed owner. But before this something even more terrible had happened. He was woken up and was preparing to say "Click!" as usual, when Stelios's fingers took him and placed him, upright, between the open legs of his mistress, then slowly drew him up and down a few times, while she half laughed and half groaned. He felt himself drowning, being extinguished. It was not so much painful as terrifying; and when he was finally put back upright on the chest of drawers he realized that his throat was blocked up by moisture and that he would not be able to speak any more. And yet! Three minutes later, when Miss Penny had left the room, Lambrinos took him in his hand and, after first smelling him, turned his little wheel round a bit – and he discovered that as if by magic he was able to speak and to light as before. Then he was lost in the pocket of a man's jacket that was hanging on the wardrobe key.

He soon realized that his fortune was made; for from time to time his new master used to take him to be refilled at the kiosk in the square; this operation was a trifle painful but was worth it. After so many adventures he finally acquired a name of his own to distinguish him from all the others. Now and then Lambrinos would lift him to his nose and smell him, but a long time had passed and he no longer smelt of anything. It seems, though, that his master had some way of remembering the scent by himself, and that Yellow Fellow served as the spark which ignited his memory; and Stelios would sometimes groan, "I want it" and sometimes "I like it" and sometimes (changing his voice so that it seemed more womanish) would sigh, "Oh Penny".

After the day's work Stelios, who was unmarried and without any steady relationship, needed a little company. Friends he had – he was easy to get on with and was happy with anything: a bit of drinking, a bit of eating, a little football, a little sex ("the old man never says no to anything!") – there were no fixed days for any of these, just whatever cropped up. He would pick up the phone: whoever said "Right!" Lambrinos would answer "You're on!" He'd get dressed and at about eight would walk down the quiet street to the square – if the friends he was meeting were from home ground – or would get the trolley bus if they were from other territory; he avoided driving at night.

His old mother kept the drawers full of clean, well ironed clothes, fragrant with the inimitable smell of home laundry which for him was his mother's secret – something entirely her own which one day (perish the thought) would be lost along with her. He wasn't too bothered about clothes: they were all just garments, after all, and if we have to cover up our bodies with something, then this one here would serve as well as that one there. Only for the office did he take any trouble; Kouvelas told him that it didn't do to meet clients looking like the greengrocer's errand boy, so Stelios had acquired one or two outfits which he wore only for the office. His moustache was also part of this disguise. He had ordered it from Kapsali's. But as time went by, his office clothes began to be a burden. In the old days he used to change when he got home. Recently he had started taking his burnous with him and changing at the office. All his attempts to give a personal touch to this part of his life (to receive clients barechested in summer, or to call them "old man" and to confide in them his sexual preferences) had failed in the face of the powerful opposition of Petros and Minas.

It was obvious, anyway, that the single factor to which the office owed its success was precisely its showcase appearance: the beautiful secretary, the perfect manners of Kouvelas and Restis, the distance from the client that they maintained, the insistence that all typed documents should be perfect, without the smallest mistake, as good as printed, the office stationery, the special folders that they gave to clients containing all the documents of the case and the bill. The "For Professional Services" drawn up – exclusively – by Kouvelas used to make Stelios hold his breath. Each time he was afraid that the client would break out into expletives. It had never happened. The larger the amount, the quicker they would pay it, and the less likely it was that they would start haggling over it. And there was a way Petros had of getting up people's noses: "My dear Mr. Fokianos, instead of making you a better price, as you suggest, I would much rather charge you nothing for our services. It might mean that we'd lose our expenses, but we would certainly gain your gratitude."

Mr. Fokianos (who had thirteen vessels at sea and a wife at home even more degenerate than his daughter) got angry at the beginning and vanished. But four months later he reappeared, full of complaints about lawyers who didn't know their own job (he had in the meantime gone to another law firm that they knew) "and it would be better not to say more so as not to damage anyone's reputation" and so on. Petros had raised his eyebrows à la Clark Gable.

"Your lawyer knows his business very well, Mr. Fokianos," he said. "He doesn't, however, know the things that we know even though it's not our business." (The client froze.)

Where does the bastard get it from, thought Stelios with admiration. Well, so be it. Fokianos had been their best customer since then. He paid the amount outstanding as well as the new bill and there was never any further word about their fees.

"Dig it!"

The coca-cola can was empty. He shuffled to his feet like a bear and went to throw it in the rubbish bin. His mother may have been a saint, but she was an obsessive housewife. She didn't want rubbish lying around. And Stelios, who couldn't see the nose on his face without his glasses, tended to scatter rubbish right and left, and she shouted at him (part of her plan to make him not feel disadvantaged, perhaps?).

The telephone rang in the hall. "Who could it be?" he wondered, still holding the empty coca-cola can ready to throw away.

"Kouvelas!" answered the can, in a last attempt to be useful, as it fell into the bin. Objects always learn more quickly than us, for they keep their ears open all the time and do not divide the world into animate and inanimate things. Within seconds the news had been transmitted from Nea Kambara to Batané by the plants on Kouvelas's balcony and the creeper that grew up the building from the garden to Lulu who was standing parked at the kerb, and from Lulu to his passing colleagues who passed it instantly from mouth to mouth to the trolley buses at the terminus in Batané Square. The trolley buses told it to one of those green three-wheeled colleagues of theirs, who whistled it in passing to the gerbera which Stelios's mother kept and cosseted on the window sill by the front door, and she passed it on into the house. Marmaro had fallen asleep and didn't hear anything.

However, Stelios had to lift the receiver in order to find out who it was. Petros's voice was hurried, his manner anxious. Minas had called him a few minutes ago and had told him that he was in the Wireless area on the trail of Betsy. She had been stolen from outside his house. Various informers whom he didn't name had indicated a place and a suspect. He needed reinforcements quickly.

"But what can we do?" asked Stelios.

"Put on your moustache, in any case," said Petros. "Do you know the Wireless area at all?"

"No, I never had any dealings down there."

"Well, ask your way and get to the Constantinople, don't forget that. I'll be waiting for you by the kiosk in Koutloumousiou Square. Shall we say in half an hour?"

"Half an hour! With the washtub! And in this traffic!

You can count yourself lucky if I'm there in an hour from now ... if not more," said Stelios. "You know that it's difficult for me and that I never drive at night, for fuckinghellsake.... And I had defused!"

"A true friend shows up in the hour of need," said Kouvelas.

"Shove it," said Stelios and hung up.

He went into the bedroom, put on socks and shoes, then threw his cigarettes, his wallet and Yellow Fellow into his bag and picked up Marmaro's keys. Before leaving he left a note for his mother saying that he'd be eating out that night.

ALL DAY THEY HAD BEEN LOITERING AROUND. Before God brought the light of day, as if summoned by bugle call, ten or fifteen of them had already gathered near the Customs or the Station, depending on where they'd been sleeping. In summer problems were few; and in this God-given land eight of the twelve months were summer. They took life easy. Finding food was no problem. The older ones among them remembered the stories of hunger and misery which their parents had told them, but they seemed to belong to a remote past, as unreal as fairy tales. Disease, police cars, dog catchers, poisoners – these days they only figured in the stories recounted as the gang huddled in a warm corner of a café or behind a tavern stove in wintertime. In the present day world people have enough and to spare, they're not mean – there's always food left over which gets thrown away; no, this was not something they had to worry about. If you knew the right places you could always take on ballast at any hour of the day; and then you could stretch out in the shade or wander through the streets gossiping and gawping, or you could go and find the gang if you had a mind to conversation and company. The places they hung out were all well known; if you didn't find them in one place you'd succeed in another. Among the girls there was Roula, Vangelitsa, Marmo and Bilio, Ketara and Maniatissa. Among the boys there was Thymios, Thodoras and Thanassis, Costas, Cosmas and Kyriakos, Mentis, Memas and Mitsos whom they used to call Arsehole because of his morals, Savvas, Sotiris and Stathis and many more – once upon a time thirty or even forty kids could get together at any one time.

They set out from the Customs and, going up Harilaos Trikoupis Street came out at Pashalimani to stand and stare at the yachts and the girls, they went up from Kastella or they lay around at the Skylitsio Theatre, they made their way towards Faliron and watched the fairground or the circus: there was always something worth seeing over there, by the Karaiskaki Stadium. You could get into conversation or tell jokes with the weird animals feeding in their cages, whose strange smell wasn't like anything you'd ever come across before. If you approached them right and managed to start chatting, you could learn a lot. But not all of them were in the mood for conversation. The large animals were rather silent. Cosmas used to like looking at the tigers and panthers. They were silent and ungiving, measuring you up through their half-closed eyelids. The eyes of a panther behind bars could make you wiser in a single minute than a whole lifetime of listening to your elders who knew so much.

Others of them preferred football. Since they had free

right of entry they'd go into the stadium and cast a glance at the game and at the mosaic of sports fans who made the tiers look like a giant multi-coloured rag rug hanging on the wall. But those who liked football were few, and were mostly the younger ones: Thymios, Mentis and Memas were the most ardent fans; the rest couldn't stand the noise and the shouting and the bother; Kyriakos had once begun to be interested in football and had had the idea that they should organize themselves into teams – but then one day he had chanced to be at the stadium at the end of the game, just as the spectators were starting to leave. He got away by the skin of his teeth and never went anywhere near a ball game again.

They had a much better relationship with the Hippodrome. They liked horses; the horses were always calm and polite – they spoke in low voices and smelled lovely. You might well say that they were the true athletes: when they ran it seemed to have a purpose. In their free time the gang set out a course and raced each other, either for speed on the flat or with obstacles for jumping. And the Hippodrome, too, was better than the stadium as a place to hang out: it had places where you could stretch out, and shade and tranquillity, it had trees and walls to piss on. And when people came there were some beautiful ladies: you could stand there and gaze at them for hours. Some of the bolder members of the gang had got friendly with women of breeding. Stathis and Thanassis had even screwed two girls right under the noses of their masters who were busy watching the course. Yes, the Hippodrome was what most of them liked best. A lot of them used to stay there overnight, keeping the racehorses company and watching with admiration the washing and grooming and feeding that they received from the stable lads. Then they'd settle down on whatever bales of straw they found in the stables and would go off to sleep, listening to the horses chewing and murmuring their stories.

At night, too, the area around the Hippodrome offered a lot to look at. Groups of men dressed as women would be hanging around on street corners, cars came and went, comments could be heard as car windows were rolled down, agreements were reached, doors opened and closed. Sometimes fights broke out between the transvestites, someone would get beaten up, hair would be pulled out, rivals would be rolling on the ground. Each one had his own spot, not trespassed upon by others. Lots of them were accompanied and placed there by their protectors who sub-leased the spot from some more important gentleman; these protectors used to step back out of sight and watch the goings on. Whenever a transvestite returned to his position he had to hand over his takings at once; for even they themselves did not like carrying cash on them.

One of these money collectors was Mr. Manthos, whose appearance and general demeanour was that of a respectable householder. Mr. Manthos had a soft spot for the gang and every evening he always brought something for them; he had a small plastic pouch – like a big purse – into which went the takings and out of which came various tasty morsels for his friends.

The transvestites spoke a beautiful language compared to other people. For example, they used to call the gang "wolfies" and "fidelios", and you'd have to be a human not to understand how much more suitable these names were than the one that people usually use.

So these strange people used to get in and out of cars, to come and go, to withdraw with their lovers behind the wall of the Hippodrome or into the open-air car park at the Delta where the boulevard began, or they left to go to hotels or to a private bachelor pad if their client was wealthy. The gang would stand at the side and watch until the market began to quiet down and the to-ings and fro-ings became less. Those who were in the mood for it would set off along the coast to Kalamaki* to watch the kids on motorbikes. Those who didn't like the noise would take the inner roads towards the Wireless or Nea Kambara Square. The air would be full of smells from early on and most of them – accustomed to eating in the evening – would set their course accordingly.

Tonight, three of the gang had started making their way up the slight slope towards the Wireless area, drawn by the incomparable fragrance of goat meat that wafted towards them, making them drool. In silence, for hunger had suddenly got the better of them as they played under the eucalyptus trees by the stables, heads down, tails lowered – a sign that they were on their way somewhere specific and didn't feel like stopping on the way or getting into conversation or scentings with strangers – they lolloped along briskly, taking the shortest route, their nostrils flaring as they followed the invisible fragrant thread which came and went with differing intensity from one street to another. In Moreos Street, a dark and deserted little alley just before Koutloumousiou Square, they had to squeeze single file onto the pavement as a taxi came up behind them and overtook them, raising a cloud of dust and

* A suburb of Athens.

leaving the stink of its exhaust right in their faces.

"Bad cess to you," growled Thodoras.

"A priest! It's bad luck!" said Mitsos the Arsehole.

They pulled up short. Inside the taxi could indeed be seen the black robe which as the brake lights came on had bent forward towards the driver. The door opened and the bearded man, swathed in his black drapes, got out carefully, holding under his arm a small black wallet – "just like Mr. Manthos's," commented Cosmas, a young black and white fellow whose gaze was as dark as a cat's.

"Can anyone guess what the other thing he's carrying is?" he challenged.

They stood a few steps away, pricking up their ears. The priest was holding the sacrament, covered with a red cloth, taking care not to spill it. He looked up at the house then told the taxi driver to wait.

"You won't be too long now, will you, Father?" said the driver in a sugary tone. "This is the busiest time of day for me, and we've got three kids at home to feed."

"I'm only just going to give one communion," the priest answered, "if he hasn't already died, then I'll be right back."

"Soup!" suggested Mitsos and Cosmas burst out laughing.

"Listen, mate, what do you expect, we haven't had much to do with priests and we're not used to all that stuff. I can hear perfectly clearly that it's liquid and goes slip-slop. If it isn't soup, then it must be.... Wait, I've had an idea.... Move it round a bit more, you old scare-crow!..."

As the priest stood upright on the pavement in front of them, the smell came across clearly.

"Wine!" said Mitsos.

"Yes, I'll tell you so that you know, they give it to humans before they kick the bucket," said Cosmas with authority – for he had once spent a short season living in a deacon's house.

"Beat it, mongrels!" said the priest.

The dogs had blocked his way as they spread out over the pavement to have a look at him and he was feeling uneasy.

"Beat it! Out of my way!"

"It's a public right of way," growled Mitsos contemptuously.

"Beat it! Beat it dirty dogs...."

"You look dirty yourself, you old goat...."

"Damned animals, go to hell! Beat it."

The taxi driver got out of the car to give his assistance to the priest, stamping and waving his arms threateningly.

"Get out of the way, fuckingdamndogs!"

Alarmed by the rough shouts, the gang gave way and went back down the road, opening up the priest's path to the house.

"Thank you," the priest said to the taxi driver, "if I'd had my hands free I would have managed myself. But tell me, do you think this house is number three? I can't see any number on the door."

"It must be three, Father," said the driver who was at least twice as old as the priest. "It doesn't say so, but that one there is number one and the street doesn't have any other houses to start with...."

"Why can't these good people put the number on the door?" said the priest. "It's not very nice to knock at the wrong door when you're carrying the sacrament."

“I’ll knock if you like, Father,” said the taxi driver who didn’t understand the delicacy of the priest’s train of thought.

Still laughing and coughing, the gang continued to make its way towards the goat fragrance. Two streets further on the scent had become so intense that you almost felt it was already in your mouth. It was coming from Koutloumousiou Square, and surely from the grill-house called “Thraka”.

“Back into Gabriel’s territory, whether you like it or not,” Thodoras teased Mitsos. “That cat, for chrissake. You can’t go a single week without seeing him.”

“Tonight there are lots of us,” said Mitsos frowning, “he won’t appear.”

The wound above his left eyebrow had only just healed. The stupid cat had a weird obstinacy which made him refuse to budge from in front of the kitchen door, even when he had eaten his fill and was stuffed with food. Cats act as if they own the place; no dog who had already eaten would block the way to a hungry colleague, or even a cat. Mitsos had taken quite a beating, but he’d also got a few blows in as well.

The noise from the square became louder; lights were coming from the street corners. They got into single file like a patrol, which is what they always did in inhabited areas in order not to provide a target. At the end of the street just before the square a garland of lighted bulbs made a play of colour: red, yellow, blue. Beneath them was a brightly lit entrance, and from within came the rhythmic beat of music. They hung back a little, while Mitsos pissed on a lamppost and Thodoras and Cosmas on a wall, then they drew a bit nearer to listen to the music and to have a look from the entrance at whatever there was to be seen.

A young man in stylish trousers, his belt slung low over his hips and his hair carelessly flopping over his forehead then growing longer at the back so that it covered the neck of his partly unbuttoned shirt. A girl, shorter than him, wearing cheaply stitched mocassins decorated with multicoloured leather circles and tassels. He held her imprisoned between his sunburnt arms, leaning forward with his palms against the red wall by the entrance.

"And I told my mum that I'd do my English homework tonight," the girl said decisively. "So what?"

Thodoras cleared his throat as a sign to the others to prick up their ears, then sat on his haunches. Cosmas and Mitsos copied him.

"It's not the same thing!" said the boy, "it's not the same thing at all."

"Of course it is. Who did you promise?"

"Myself!" said the boy, with a hint of desperation in his voice. "Look: I took my cousin's bike so that we could go for a ride together."

He pointed to Betsy on the pavement. Who, bright red and shiny, was looking around anxiously; she had heard from two-wheeled and two-stroke colleagues (these were what circulated all round her in this unknown neighbourhood) that Minas was searching all through Athens for her.

"A ride!" said the girl mockingly. "And who gave you that idea? A ride, the two of us together! So that's where we're at, is it?"

"I want to," said the boy obstinately.

"The younger they are, the more difficult," commented Cosmas, who had also fallen for young girls.

"And I'm supposed to leave my homework to go for a ride with you? Is that what you think? That I can waste my free time so that you can do wheelies?"

"You can't do wheelies with this one, this is a serious bike."

The girl refused to listen. She removed the boy's arms from either side of her and put them where they belonged as if they were two planks of wood.

"If you said going dancing, yes. Going to bed, yes. But not going for a ride – and with a stolen bike into the bargain! In the evening, just like Romeo and Juliet! Something that would clear the homework from my brain, OK. If you want us to have a threesome with Lena, let's go."

"I can't stand Lena! I've told you, I'm sick of her! I don't get off that way. I hate it."

"Well, that's the only way I get off," said the girl. "Anyway, what's happened all of a sudden that you're sick of her?"

"I'm sick of sharing you with her."

"Sharing me? And who ever told you that Lena likes sharing you with me? Did you ever bother to ask? Oh no! Master Soulis is a big greedy egoist. He's just like all men, he wants to put a stamp on women, those who belong to him and those who don't.... Love is a free choice, my lad! It's about time you learnt that...."

"If she was a bitch, I'd like her to be the mother of my children," murmured Thodoras with his eyes half closed.

The boy pleaded with her in vain, saying her name over and over. The girl suddenly detached herself from the wall and disappeared into the depths of the disco. Lightheaded from the unexpected way things had gone, the gang only just had time to get out of the way as Soulis strode forward onto the pavement, sighing and searching for his crumpled packet of cigarettes. The world seemed to have quaked under his feet. Thoughts of revenge clouded his mind. Voula said no to him more often than to Lena. So he wasn't strong or attractive enough, he wasn't worth anything as a man – yet everyone, both boys and girls, said how handsome Soulis was. But all girls are abnormal perverts – liberation had gone to their heads. How could she prefer pussy rubbing with Lena to his own manly embrace? No – it was his own fault. His embrace was not manly enough. Because if it was, then she would give in to him instantly. It was his fault, quite simply his fault. Tears of anger filled his eyes.

"I'll never understand humans," said Cosmas.

"PETROS," SAID VERONICA KOUVELAS to her husband, "are you going to go off and leave your doe and little fawns alone again?"

"Darling, you say it as if it was fun for me to go out again, I've hardly even got back from the office."

He sighed, and continued putting on clothes that barely fitted him. He had put on weight again.

Hypocrisy or honesty – it all depends on the prism through which you look at it; prism, prism, prison, prissy.

"They won't do up, sweetheart, these damned trousers that we bought from your school friend's boutique which is going broke won't do up," he said smiling.

The children were receiving a non-authoritarian

upbringing. And the parents were both cool and enlightened people – professionals.

"It's because you've been eating like you used to, dearest, imagining that you are still in your family cradle" said Veronica Kouvelas, and she lifted up her younger son Andreas who had asked to be picked up by an unintelligible string of vowels.

"Since I've got to put them on, tell me how to do it," asked Petros, "I remember that there's some trick."

"Yes. Lie down on the bed, your stomach will subside a bit and you can pull the zip up."

"I knew it had something to do with gravity," he said, and set off barefoot over the corridor carpet towards the bedroom.

As he passed the open door of his study, he saw his elder son Argyris painting with water colours on the spine of his best briefcase.

"So what was that story you were telling me?" asked Veronica, who had brought Andreas in her arms to the door of the bedroom so that he could watch his father getting dressed lying down.

"It isn't a story," said Kouvelas, trying to get up. "Minas says that Betsy – his motorcycle – has been stolen and that he's on the tracks of the thief in the Wireless area. And that he hasn't notified the police because he's with his uncle, the general, and the thief is someone his uncle knows and they want to avoid scandal."

"I didn't know that she was called Betsy," said Veronica, "nor that Minas had an uncle who's a general."

"Retired."

"Just as well." Mrs. Kouvelas put Andreas down.

"Babouma," said Andreas.

"Of course, darling," said his mother. "Go and find Argyris and play Bow-bow with him."

"Bayo," said Andreas, "Bayo-bouma."

"Whatever you want, darling" said Veronica.

"Gow Bayo," said Andreas firmly and went to find Argyris.

"I'm afraid that I'll die before I hear a single comprehensible word from our offspring," said Petros, searching in the wardrobe for his shoes.

"That's not surprising at all. Grown-ups never understand children anyway," said his wife.

"All right, at what age do non-authoritarian children learn to talk?"

"At whatever age they like," she said. "What are you looking for?"

"Where are my shoes?" said Petros, kneeling with his head inside the wardrobe. "I'll drop dead and they won't be able to get me out of these trousers."

"How terrible. But surely you won't be needing to take them off before you get back tonight."

He put his shoes on, sitting on the bed. When he had done so he was bright red; all the blood had gone to his head.

I'm glad to be going out again so soon, though I do my best not to show it. I look as if I'm annoyed, grumbling, wretched. It's all part of the usual performance. But I'm "obliged" to give support to my friend in his trouble – thus I've got an excuse. Hypocrisy or honesty: in the last analysis everything is coloured by the inner needs of our superego. What are the things we suppress every day, and what are the things we allow to burst forth freely? We wouldn't recognize our own lives if we saw them made into a film.... What have we managed to learn? Nothing. Temptations only and inhibitions.

"I'm thinking that I don't know anything about Minas, anything about Stelios, about the office, about your life there every day," said Veronica.

"There's nothing much worth mentioning. Our life begins when we come home from the office," said Petros tritely.

On his way out of the apartment his wife straightened his thinning hair which was sticking out in all directions. She had already asked him twice if he would be late. He did not know. How could he tell? He was honest. Honest and with a good excuse. Happy, that is to say. Veronica thought about how much she didn't know about him.

"Betsy...." she began timidly, fidgeting with the buttons on his shirt, "have you ever ridden on her?"

"Once or twice," he confessed reluctantly.

This was a lie, of course; he had never ridden Betsy. Create suspicions yourself where they don't do the other person any good, Kouvelas had taught his younger colleagues. And tell whichever parts of the truth there isn't any reason for hiding. An out-and-out lie is like a castle without a moat. Always try to distinguish the things which it doesn't matter telling.

"Addio amore," he said to his wife and slipped into the lift.

He goes out and says "that's done – now I'm going down like a deus ex machina, knowing that my good luck will bring everything right and the affair will have a happy ending ... and Veronica is staying with Andreas and Argyris – to be optimistically tyrannized by the results of a anti-authoritarian upbringing – what rubbish."

"I feel guilty, Lulu," he said as he started the car. "Guilty. Do you know what that is? A kind of malfunction. Like when your distributor goes wrong. Guilty that when I am with you I feel so happy. Guilty that I had children. Guilty when I didn't have them. D'you think, in the end, that other people are happier than we imagine them to be? Do you think that in reality they're happier than we think we can make them? What do we owe ourselves and others, Lulu? I'm putting the question to you, and I'd like your answer as a machine. All right, for example Minas: he phones me and wants me to help him. What does he really expect me to do? He knows perfectly well that I don't have the sort of skills needed for this job. For example Veronica: she imagines that I react like all fathers everywhere, with secret admiration for our offspring – she who once knew me so well; and I live with the fear that one day she'll realize that I don't care about anything but myself – not the children and not her. I've got to live my whole life from now on acting the part of a man who tries to camouflage the explosive outbursts of his feelings; to joke, to be sarcastic, to be cold, to absent myself as often as possible – but with a good excuse, like a schoolboy staying away from school. Having to bring the signature of a parent or guardian. To fool people or be fooled ceaselessly. No, it doesn't bother me, don't think that. It's an enormous pleasure to observe the variety, the thousand details of all these deceptions. At the office, let's say for example, Vipsy is a bit smitten with Minas. But Minas is more or less engaged and Vipsy knows Evanthitsa – they've gone out together. Thus Vipsy goes with me, as well as with Stelios, so that she can also go with Minas 'neutrally'. That's as far as her mind works.... Or, again, take Penny

Karakoulia. Penny used to go out with Stelios. However they had an accommodation problem. So they used to use my bachelor flat. One evening when Stelios left first, I arrived and found Penny there. Penny fancied me right from the beginning and began to play the same trick systematically. One of us would leave and the other would arrive. After a while Penny confesses to Stelios that she is in love with someone else and breaks off with him. And I, who in the meantime have been pretending deep feeling with Penny, become at the same time Stelios's confidant, and together we rail at the inconstancy and the calculating ways of women. Poor Stelios! Unsuspecting and full of willingness to share everything with his friends, he introduces me to his two Freaks, Christinaki and Errikoula. And at the same time Mairoula – Fokianos's secretary – begins to join in the fun, believing that I am a stunning case of a left-wing intellectual trapped by the prejudices of my social class, by my marriage which oppresses me and by the System which I am obliged to serve in order to live. As the wise machine that you are, what would you do, Lulu? Would you laugh or would you cry?"

Petros drove at medium speed in order to listen to the calm purring of the engine, enjoying the obedient changes of the gearbox, the immediate and dulcet way in which Lulu responded to his steering wheel which Petros caressed as one might caress the head of a faithful animal. Dear Lulu, he said to him every so often. And Lulu purred like a tom-cat. "OK," he said, "you're OK."

He stopped at a kiosk. He asked how to get to Koutloumousiou Square. The kiosk man was a war veteran wearing a hearing aid whose batteries had run low. He wasn't used to giving directions to passers-by.

"I don't have any, I've run out," he said.

Two or three blocks further down, two girls were walking arm in arm. He slowed and put his head out of the window.

"Excuse me...."

"Lena, he's all yours," the girl with the decorated mocassins warned her friend.

"Well really, come out kerb-crawling with the baby seat still in the back of the car, have you, grandad?" said Lena angrily to Petros. "What decrepit old carcasses one does run into these days, friend."

The two girls quickened their pace and moved off. Kouvelas looked in the rear mirror at Andreas's baby seat and shook his head. He drove ahead to catch them up.

"I'm looking for Koutloumousiou Square, Miss, you misunderstood me."

"Just listen to that, you old satyr! If you don't get out of here at once I'll start screaming."

And, without waiting even a second, the girl began to scream so loud that her eyes almost popped out of her head.

Cursing all generations younger than his own, Petros put his foot down on the accelerator and immediately took a turning into another road. He came out into the square.

It was a typical working-class neighbourhood square, with a kiosk at one end, in the middle a useless little park with various shrubs dotted around an incomprehensible statue aiming its point heavenwards like an outstretched finger. All round the square were the usual everyday shops: a bakery, a milk shop, a grill-house, a café, a chemist. The disco was near the corner of the road opposite the kiosk, the flashes of the lights round the entrance reaching half way across the square. On the other corner, by the milk shop, was the bus terminus.

He parked Lulu at the kerb and cast a searching eye around. Neither Minas nor Stelios was to be seen. It was late – nothing new can begin at such an hour, things are already in the middle of happening.... Ancient problems – modern dramas.

Three dogs turned the corner by the disco and sat on the pavement, looking over the square and casting furtive glances at the grill-house. The fragrant smoke was brimming over the top of the chimney and at the entrance to the courtyard a large white cat possessing half an ear was washing himself with slow movements. Petros's gaze wandered uncertain, abstracted, from the cat to the dogs and then back again; but he could not understand any of the messages that were coming and going from one end of the square to the other.

"Petros!"

"Minas!"

His friend was standing beside him at the car window, leaning with his hands on the rolled down glass. He was bright red from emotion. He explained rapidly. His uncle had set out alone from the square "to find some people he knew who would help". Father Rostis was asleep in the car – the evening's excitements had proved too much for him.

"Poor old man," said Minas.

"Never mind," said Petros, "mine has been in a permanent coma since the day he was twenty-one. So what do we do till your uncle gets back?"

"Our own investigation!" Minas answered with

enthusiasm. "This is what we know so far. Our man is called Soulis."

"Soulis – short for Thanassis?"

"Soulis. You never know with these popular names. It might be short for Zervas, Sakelarios or Venizelos. He's eighteen, medium height, brown hair over his forehead in front and longer at the back, covering his collar. Light honey-coloured eyes, hairless wheat-coloured skin, straight nose, probably small, red fleshy lips, thick white teeth ('Dig it,' said Petros). Narrow waist. Modern clothes. This evening he was wearing a long-sleeved blue shirt with the sleeves rolled up to his elbows, dark brown trousers with a low waist, tight fitting over his thighs. Canvas sports shoes with various colours on them. He always wears a bracelet with his name on it and a white bone necklace."

"And you haven't even seen him," said Petros. "We could start by asking at the café, I should think. Someone in the neighbourhood must know him."

Minas looked worried and a bit fraught. Uncle Stefanos had forbidden his nephew to follow him. He had been furious when Minas told him that he had called his friends to hurry to their aid. He seemed as if he had brought Minas here more to keep an eye on his movements than to help him in the search. He had cloaked everything in deep mystery from then onwards. He was "certain" that he would sort it out alone. He was "certain" that Minas and Iolaos Restis should stay in the square by the car and "not move from there, nor his friends either when they arrived", that "his acquaintances would at once be able to give him all the necessary information to find the motorcycle surely and without delay", because "he held a strong hand of cards, concerning all of them and each one separately". With these vague promises Uncle Stefanos had left them and had disappeared.

"QUIET," SIGNED THODORAS SILENTLY.

They had come round the square and were approaching the entrance to the courtyard. Gabriel had finished washing and was sitting on top of the wall above the door, on the pillar, like a small lime-washed clay statue.

"We don't want to cause trouble," said Cosmas. "One piece each, and we'll take them and eat them outside...." The big cat couldn't object to that.

Gabriel remained motionless.

"We'll keep our word" said Thodoras, "our good faith in return for yours, cat."

They made a small step forwards.

"Entrance prohibited" said Gabriel.

The dogs froze.

"Entrance is forbidden, to strangers."

"I didn't hear anything," said Cosmas, "Thodoras, did you hear anything?"

"I didn't either."

"Entrance is completely forbidden," said Gabriel. "And for those who have entered, exit will be forbidden."

A shiver passed through the dogs.

"Don't you think you're going a bit far, mate," said Mitsos, "there are three of us and only one of you. And anyway, are you a he or a she? I don't know how many holes you have under your fur."

"As many as I need," replied the cat, "unlike you

who, as they say, look as if you could do with one or two more."

"Come down here!" shouted Mitsos, beside himself (can't let cats insult our manhood).

"I'll come down," said Gabriel, "when it's time to do so."

The dogs looked at one another; they were trying to work out whether he was putting on an act or whether he was speaking seriously. A waiter emptied a couple of plates onto the heap of leftovers.

"A new delivery, boys," said Thodoras. "Leave the cat to pretend he's a statue and come and eat."

They turned their backs on the entrance and went into the courtyard. Among the bones you could find whole portions of meat: half-eaten chops, lamb cutlets with only the finest bit eaten, whole meatballs left uneaten on the plate. You only had to reach down and take it. Since they wanted to show that they kept their word, each of them only took whichever bit looked nicest and they returned immediately to the door.

Gabriel was blocking the doorway. It was clear that he wasn't joking.

PETROS AND MINAS BEGAN TO GO UP and down the shops in the square asking about Soulis. People looked at them oddly, suspiciously. The locals did not seem to be at all willing to talk to strangers; neither of them looked like a policeman, but nor did they look like anyone from any of the gangs known in the neighbourhood. They looked like extraterrestrials. Many people appeared not even to understand the language the two friends were speaking when they described the boy they were looking for. They looked up from their card games with a blank expression, or they didn't even seem to notice their presence: they went on throwing the dice and continued their conversation or their silence, the way one does when one doesn't want to buy a lottery ticket or when one is not at all tempted by the chewing gum which gypsy children try to sell. In the end, just before the friends gave up in complete despair, one of the natives seemed to be better travelled than the rest and showed some interest in their quest. A Soulis – who looked like this and this – lived a bit further down, just a few streets from the square, he said. He gave them the name of the street and the number.

Moreos Street was the third one at right angles to the street where the bus stopped. Darkness reigned. The street lamps had served as targets for all the slings and air guns of the neighbourhood – they were all dark except for one which, almost defunct from old age, threw a feeble yellowish light at the corner, just enough to read the name of the street. Number three must be further down. For next to the house which must be number one was a small triangular space, planted with bushes and little humble trees – the point where two other narrow streets met which started from Moreos Street and led away into the depths of the Wireless quarter. Total darkness. Like number one, number three – if it was three – didn't have any number outside. It was a two-storey house with an iron gate at the side, open; there was a light in the passage and at the back a dark courtyard could be made out. The entrance to the ground floor from the passage. Stairs leading to the upper floor. They agreed on their plan of action by sign language.

Petros would take the ground floor and Minas the upstairs. Before they separated they cast a quick eye over the yard. A vine, a hand-cart, chairs with seats woven of plastic strips, a pile of tools. A wall all around separated the house from other yards. No sign of Betsy. Kouvelas stood at the entrance to the ground floor and Minas ran up the stairs with rapid silent steps.

"EXCUSE ME, AM I GOING THE RIGHT way to the Wireless?" Stelios asked in his politest voice.

"The Wireless? You've quite a way to go still, lad. Go on a bit and then ask again in the centre. I'm a foreigner."

"You speak the lingo pretty well, though," said Lambrinos.

The foreigner sounded as if he came from Spata or Koropi.*

Squeaking and sighing, Marmaro went on, searching the uphill road ahead of her with her weak headlights. The air coming through the windows was cool and refreshing – colder than usual at this time of year. Man, some neighbourhoods this godforsaken city has gotten itself these past years. The Wireless, he says. Stelios had been exhausted by the time he managed to make his way out of the traffic in the centre of town. His eyes did not help at all; and concentrating intensely had given him a headache. But the fresh air of the countryside was making him feel a bit better now. Driving along at forty

* Towns situated within 25 kilometres from the centre of Athens.

kilometres an hour on the open, empty road, he felt a certain security, more than in the crowded streets of the city. He decided to treat himself to a cigarette to relax and fumbled blindly in his bag lying open on the seat beside him. His hands knew their own way, they could perform miracles in the dark (this is how he liked to see it), having necessarily had to acquire the experience of the half-blind. The cigarette packet fell back into its place and Yellow Fellow was brought out. "Click!" he said. For an instant Stelios's eyes were dazzled by the flame – just long enough for him to miss seeing a sign which passed alongside the deux chevaux, unobserved by any of them. ("All right, all right," it said, rather obstinately.)

Lights at the end of the road. A turn and they were gone. Another turn – and they seemed nearer. The centerycentre. The centre that the "foreigner" said. The deux chevaux went up on the edge of the road, its wheels spinning a bit on the gravel as it braked – dampness always made them lock.

People sitting round at tables, light from naked bulbs, the inevitable smell of food. Stelios's stomach rumbled painfully. The fragrance, in the clean mountain air, was more tempting than ever. And it was late, and he'd already had a lot of trouble and the road was dark and the end unknown. Stelios was hungry, hungry as he had rarely been. But, well, we've only got one Minas! Won't we help our friend in his need and trouble? And our friend has only got one Betsy. And one Evanthitsa.

"And a third of Vipsy," muttered Lambrinos between his teeth; hunger had a strange way of combining itself with the prickings of his sexual instinct.

The waiter stopped for a moment and looked him

over from top to toe, balancing two tiers of plates for the dishwasher on his arms. In his mouth a toothpick.

"Straight ahead mate to the big junction ask again anyway turn left and look to the right. Comprenny?"

"Comprenny," said Lambrinos who hadn't understood anything except that he still had some way to go. Shrugging his shoulders fatalistically he went back to Marmaro. Straightaheady – that's the main thing, and ask againy. The Wireless is a big mystery, at any rate. The Wirelessers kept it well hidden (or should that be Wirelessters?). I bet it is illegal, like those which unpatriotic folk used to send information to Tashkent once upon a time. ("Courage, mon vieux!" he cried out to himself, once more enthusiastic. "Glory lies before us. Repose lies behind us!")

"Click!" said Yellow Fellow again.

How many more cigarettes' worth of road still ahead....

"I'm beginning to get tired," said Marmaro who had overheated as a result of going along all the time in second and third gear (for safety's sake). Yellow Fellow, stretched out comfortably on the passenger seat and overcome by an unstoppable fit of chattiness, explained to her all about Betsy's disappearance, Petros Kouvelas's phone call and the way in which their master rushed to help his friends. Marmaro was terribly upset. Poor Betsy! she said again and again. Poor Betsy! How many dangers a girl faces in today's world....

The junction lay at the bottom of a long hill. The brakes would burn if they went on much further. Stelios put his head out of the window – not to see (there was no question of this) but to listen: and the sound of the sea reached his ears quite clearly.

Funny. Let's ask that mule driver.

"Evenin', friend!" he said in a rustic accent.

"Prrr!" said the man on the mule and the animal stopped.

"Oi be trying to get to t'Woireless. Be oi going roight?"

The other man bent down curiously, trying to get a look at him in the dark.

"Ugh!" he said.

"Be oi on t'roight road for t' Woireless? Be it a long way furrther?" shouted Stelios as if he thought the man was hard of hearing.

"Ugh-urr!" said the man.

"Roight or left? Because straight in front oi do hear the sea.... Roight?"

"Ugh-urr!"

"Left?"

"Ugh!"

"Thanks, friend," sighed the traveller and put the car into first gear.

"Amazing what hillbillies Athens seems to be full of these days," said the mule man to himself as he spurred the beast and disappeared into the darkness.

Shadows of eucalyptus trees passed him; then open land stretched out, running down to the sea – fields and wasteland. The waiter had said so: left at the junction and look right. Suddenly he saw it: it had to be the Wireless, no doubt about it.

Low one-storey houses with rows of windows, some of them lit and some dark under the light of the street lamps. No movement. Completely dead. It looked like a working-class neighbourhood; people must be asleep at this hour (or having it off on the beach?). And in fact what time was it anyway?

He went down a dirt track off to the right of the surfaced road until he was about a hundred metres from the first houses. Actually it didn't seem to be a very large place. He decided to leave the deux chevaux there and to go and look for his friends on foot. He locked the car and started to walk. Once or twice he stumbled on stones. He got a torch out of his bag (which he always had with him at night because in the dark he was totally blind) and continued to search the road. It looked like an agricultural area; those buildings over there looked like barns for hay – long and narrow, without windows or lights. What the hell did they call it Wireless for?

As he walked hunched up he suddenly hit his forehead on something metal which rang out loudly. Oh Jesus! he cried and rubbed his head.

"Hang on, you wanker," he called, as if talking to someone else. "Where the hell have I got to?"

It was his mind rather than his sight which had cleared, so that he began to see better.

"I put my head down and set off like a donkey. I get out of town and don't even wonder if it's possible for any neighbourhood to be so far out.... I ask someone the way who says he's German, then a waiter who talks through a toothpick and a mule man who answers 'ugh!' and 'ugh-urr!' and leaves me high and dry. And where do I get to? A cow shed. Not even that! I get to a wire fence, godforsaken fool that I am, and through it I can see checkpoints and sheds and camp buildings and radar masts and my own cuckold's horns and I sit here looking at them and I'm certain that this area is the Wireless. And I've reached the American base at Nea Pangri. That's it, boys, the base has radio! That's why they all sent me here. Stupid wanker! What have I gone and done? I'll tell them about it tomorrow in the office and they'll shit themselves laughing...."

He had sat down on the ground. At first he laughed; when he got tired of laughing he lay down on his face and started searching for his glasses which had fallen off when he hit his head. He had decided to get back into the washtub, to go back to Athens, take a taxi and go to the real Wireless quarter, no matter what time it was.

Just then he heard footsteps approaching. Heavy footsteps on the gravel. His first thought was "help finding my glasses – proper directions to find my way back out of here". However, as the footsteps came nearer, he felt that the sound had something threatening about it, threatening and inevitable.

A CLOUD OF DUST ROSE UP IN THE ENTRANCE to the small courtyard as the three friends with their heads down surged forwards to pass the barrier made by the fierce raised white fur of Gabriel who seemed to have swollen to twice his normal size. Mitsos and Cosmas managed to get through; only the chop that Cosmas was holding in his teeth fell onto the ground. Thodoras was less lucky; since he was in the middle, it was he who came to a stop with his head up against the cat's claws. Screams of pain and rage, curses and sobs intermingled. The other two came back to help their friend who was in dire straits. The food had gone, as had their appetite, hunger and good mood. Now it was war; and they were determined to put an end once and for all to the white cat's greed and terrorism. Thodoras was still fighting to escape, with the meatball in his mouth – he wasn't going to let it go. In just a few seconds Gabriel had managed to jump on him two more times. It was as if he was made of India rubber. He jumped back, stood on his hind legs and jumped forward again with eighteen claws as hooked as talons and as sharp as razors, and with all his teeth bared, while from head to tail his fur was standing up on end like a porcupine. He knew perfectly well the difference in strength between him and his enemies and was counting on the element of surprise. So far he'd succeeded. As the other dogs returned he realized he'd have to change tactics. The narrowness of the passage was in his favour: they were not as supple as him, and there were three of them, tripping over one another, getting in each other's way, stumbling.

The row was so loud that even people on the other side of the square had got up to see what was happening. The boss of the grill-house sent the waiter with a bucket of water to break it up. Meanwhile the struggle looked as if it would continue to the death. Cosmas had withdrawn to one side and was licking the warm blood that was flowing from his shoulder. Mitsos and Thodoras had managed to get Gabriel up against the wall. They were howling with anger, their throats tight. But it was a mistake to corner a cat and they knew it. Blind with fear, he hurled himself forward like a rubber ball, heedless of everything. He rarely missed his mark – be it an eye or a nose – and nothing could stop him. He spat and growled and came at them from everywhere. But the dogs were driven wild by his smell – cats at such moments give off a smell of death – their muscles hard as steel, their mouths gaping, all teeth, their eyes flashing. Gabriel hurled himself through their midst with a tremendous leap of such speed that they didn't even see it. He had marked out a spot and burrowed into it, between some empty bread bins under the bench. Reinforced now by Cosmas who had recovered sufficiently, the dogs approached the bench in a manoeuvre to cut him off once again. But at that very moment a flood of dirty water was emptied over their heads from the bucket.

In the confusion that followed Gabriel took the opportunity to escape from one side; he shot off like an arrow and climbed back up to his original position on the wall, above the door. They couldn't reach him there. Within a minute he was behaving as if nothing had happened. The dogs shook themselves and looked round in amazement for their enemy. Seeing him safe and calm up there they came up to the wall and began to swear at him in unrepeatable language in order to provoke him. Bit by bit his fur smoothed down. Then, to show them how deeply he despised them, he yawned. It was as if their curses couldn't reach him up there. What a coward, what a piece of filth, what a limp prick, they said – he said nothing. At one point he even began to wash himself. The dogs got sick of it. Their food was lying in the dust. Casting glances behind them just to be on the safe side, they went back to the pile of leftovers. Then, each with his morsel in his mouth, they left the grill-house's yard. The cat pretended not to see them.

"See you tomorrow at the same time when we come for food," said Cosmas.

"Bring a friend, why don't you?" said the cat sarcastically.

Mitsos, the last to leave, made a rude noise.

"Here's to you," he said to Gabriel.

"Watch out you don't get a prolapsed womb," replied the cat.

They ate their food lying a bit further off in a deserted street near the square. Their mood was spoilt and they no longer felt hungry.

"What a rabid cat," sighed Cosmas at one point; he had finished his food first.

"He's been knocked sideways by the menopause," said Mitsos.

The others finished their food without much enthusiasm, burped, crossed their paws.

"At any rate we sorted him out," said Thodoras. "Debts have to be paid. Next time, mark my words, he'll pretend not to see us, the tramp."

"That's what cats are like, that's the way they always were, that's the way they always will be."

As they lay there to digest and to rest a bit, they began reminiscing about cats, either their own experiences or things they had heard. Thodoras expounded his theory that there was nothing in cat behaviour that was not described in the Catiad or the Doggessey – the two arks of their oral tradition which the younger generation scorned and knew nothing of. He found plenty of examples from both epics and with his excellent memory could recite many lines to them by heart.

The two younger ones accepted that their elders knew a thing or two, and Cosmas agreed that there was nothing new under the sun which hadn't already been said. Mitsos, who was more progressive, said that anyhow young people make their own tradition and want to hear about life in their own language; that's how the world advances.

"Advances or stands still – in the end I believe it amounts to the same thing. The road uphill or downhill, it's all one road," said Thodoras conclusively.

Their mood was beginning to improve again. A marvellous thing, food. It warms the soul, makes the blood circulate more willingly through the body and good humour returns – you see everything in a more friendly light. Except for characters like Gabriel.

Just then a large group of men were coming out of the café, discussing the duel at backgammon which had taken place tonight between two old rivals: someone they called Sergopoulos and someone they called Papaniketas. The two opponents were standing in the middle of the crowd smiling; the game had ended in a draw. Sergopoulos, as he listened to the jokes, kept on and on running a comb through his glossy hair, as if he'd forgotten what he was doing or wanted to massage his scalp. Papaniketas – not to be outdone – was stuffing his shirt into his trousers, his hands like spatulas running round his belly, his sides, his arse, again and again; his shirt had been in place for some time, but the movement – which like the other man's combing expressed his satisfaction – continued. The gang stood and watched this comic sight for a while, then moved off slowly, splitting their sides with laughter.

MINAS WAITED FOR A FEW SECONDS, his ears pricked up like a hunting dog in case they should catch some sound which would make him change his plan at the last minute. He gathered all his courage and knocked twice – like a code. Evanthitsa had come into his thoughts again: he would still have been in bed with her in Petros's flat near the office, they would have finished making love, they'd be getting ready to leave, to go somewhere with

Betsy. Evanthitsa had her own helmet, the same colour as Minas's; she wore it as she sat behind him, her arms round his waist. Petros's flat – he used to have a drink and smoke as he waited for Evanthitsa. He would turn on the immersion heater, clean the ashtrays which their owner always left overflowing, air the place, turn on the fan which rotated silently back and forth on its single leg like a stork, he would light the two lamps on the table which cast such a pleasant light – and he'd be waiting, happy. Petros used to say that women are always late because they live in their own time, different from everyone else's. What might his friend be doing now? It was all Soulis's fault: the good-for-nothing little shit. Suddenly he hated him with his whole soul. He prayed that the door would open and that Soulis himself would be standing there, just as the general described him, with his locks falling on his forehead and his white bone necklace round his neck. There wouldn't be any talk, no unnecessary questions, he would just grab him and would beat him senseless. And if Betsy had come to the slightest bit of harm, he'd butcher him, he'd literally wipe him out.

He heard steps. Someone wearing slippers two sizes too large. It was a girl, about sixteen or seventeen, wearing a loose shirt, with her feet thrust into man's slippers; in one hand she held a slice of pizza and was still chewing. At the sight of Restis an expression of surprise and anxiety came over her face. It was obvious that she'd been expecting someone else. She stood in the open doorway, her question clear in her expression.

"Is Soulis here?" asked Minas.

He was almost sure that he'd hear her say that no one called Soulis lived there. The girl continued eating as she sized him up.

"Is he in?" he asked again; he was trying to get some hint from her, as fast as possible, that he was on the right track.

"No," said the girl finally.

"Where is he?" She shrugged her shoulders. His sister?

"He your brother?" he asked her.

She laughed.

"Do I look like him?"

He examined her closely; not to discover her likeness to Soulis (whom he'd never seen) but to see what sort of mood she was in. Her hair was short – like her brother's it must be; she was slim and slightly built; but her dark eyes bore witness to energy and quickness of perception. Praise be for anthropometry, thought Minas. He bent down then and noticed her thin legs with their pronounced ankles and that erotic little hollow just above the heels.

"You look like him," he said finally.

She gave a half laugh.

"What do you want?"

Minas was wondering who in the house the slippers belonged to; not her trendy brother, at any rate. Her father?

"I've got to find him," he said.

His head was bursting. Should he tell her the truth at once or some risky lie which might spoil everything?

"Where might he be at this hour?" he asked, looking as if he was trying to think.

"He might be anywhere at this hour," said the girl and laughed.

She put the bit of pizza back in her mouth, then at last stepped back so that he could pass.

"You got time to wait for him?" she asked, friendly. She appeared to have accepted him completely.

The house was clean but the furniture was hopeless. As well as supposedly "antique" pieces like the dining table and chairs, there was a white wood sofa which ended in a shelf unit with the telephone on it and the phone books decorating its three shelves; and everywhere the efforts of the younger members of the household to put their own stamp on things were plain to see: two posters were stuck to the wall with drawing pins: Rory Gallagher and a nude couple, portrayed in shadowy silhouette in front of the sea at sunset. A modern light fitting. Good quality artificial flowers in the vases: at first he had taken them for real. The corridor leading from the entrance-sitting-dining room was painted in dark brown emulsion paint. And from a room at the back came light and quiet music.

"Is anyone else here?"

"I was listening to music," said the girl, "only quietly, because we've had a death downstairs tonight." (Lucky you, Petros!)

She sat down first and signed him to sit. Minas pulled up a chair from the table and set it opposite her.

"Are you good friends with Soulis?"

"Why?"

"He's never told you about his sister?"

Minas hesitated. And now?

"I've never seen you before, anyway," she said. "Do you live at the Wireless?"

"No, I don't live here."

"I see."

"What do you see?"

"You're one of the group he goes round with...."

Minas smiled. He always smiled when he found himself in a difficult situation.

"I don't know many of his friends," said the girl. "He doesn't go about much with people from round here, they bore him. How old are you?"

"Thirty," said Minas. "And you?"

"Eighteen," said the girl, looking him in the face. "How old do I look?"

"About that," said Minas vaguely.

She offered him a cigarette.

"So what kind of people do you go around with? What sort of friends are you? And what's your name?"

"I'm called Minas," said Minas "and I've got a few things in common with your brother."

As he said this Minas was thinking of Betsy, but the girl remained silent, looking at him a little sideways, examining him.

"What are you listening to?" asked Minas to change the subject, and he nodded towards the back where the music was coming from.

"The Talking Heads," she said. "They're a bit out of date but I like them."

"In my day we listened to the Rolling Stones," said Minas. "I suppose you would consider them fossils."

"Oh no, not the Rolling Stones!" said the girl.

She had got up.

"Shall I turn it up?" she asked.

"Why don't we go to your room," said Minas.

She shrugged her shoulders and led the way. The light coming from the room with the Talking Heads silhouetted her whole body under her shirt.

The bed was a double mattress, unmade, the sheets tangled, the pillow dented – as if she had just got up from making love or from the sort of restless sleep that children have when they toss and turn in bed constantly. The floor was covered with rag rugs. The light was a Japanese lantern made of rice paper and bamboo. One wall was painted pale mauve. There were no curtains at the window – perhaps because it was summer. A large green glass demijohn, stripped of its rush covering, with two paper sunflowers. On a wooden shelf there was a small chimpanzee with a checked jockey cap; and scattered around were various stuffed toys in the form of different creatures: a hippopotamus, a frog, a little man and a large green boa, half of which was on her mattress.

"You've got a lot of friends, I see," he said to her. "Which is your best one? The snake?"

"Yes. He's Momos," answered the girl, and she went and stopped the tape. "I'll put something else on."

She took the tape out and knelt down to search through her records in a low cupboard. As he looked at her naked heels and ankles, her legs half covered by her shirt, Minas tried to make out some of the other lines of her body. Through the open window only sky could be seen; as if there was nothing at all round or near this house. He thought that he would like to be her friend. This is what he always thought when he liked someone – even with women at the beginning. She was rather ugly, in fact it was this which made him think more of friendship. She was quite a character, this girl. And her body looked very fine. Her brother must be a fine kid.

The girl took a record from its sleeve and hid it immediately so that Minas wouldn't see it. It was the Rolling Stones – an introductory offer.

"What's your name?" he asked her.

"Didn't my brother tell you that either? Gia."

"Gia. What's that short for?"

"Never you mind," she said with a laugh.

Then she put her hands on her hips and said, slightly provocatively

"Tasia. Anastasia."

"I like all three. Gia is best if you're in a hurry."

"Are you in a hurry?"

"Only to find your brother."

"Won't you stay and listen to the record?"

Minas sat down cross legged on the edge of the mattress. He gave a – mock – anxious look at Momos.

"Does he bite?"

"Sometimes," said Gia.

The girl pulled up a large cushion and sat down on the floor. Her shirt tautened and Minas, his heart beating, glimpsed the inside of two shapely thighs. Gia settled herself comfortably leaving the slippers empty at her side. Her legs were just as shapely and delicate as her arms. Evanthitsa had almost the same sort of body as Gia, but her breasts and waist came into a different, more voluptuous, category.

"Gia," said Minas, "I'll have to tell you the truth about certain things."

"IF I'VE EATEN TOO MUCH I CAN'T SLEEP. I prefer to take a little walk to help my digestion. I've been having trouble with my digestion recently," said Thodoras.

"It's because you eat too fast," said Mitsos, laughing, "you gulp your food down without chewing it."

"If you make a habit of going to restaurants like

tonight's it isn't easy...." added Cosmas laughing under his whiskers.

Koutloumousiou Square was worth looking at but it was small; as the hour got later there were fewer and fewer people about. Working people, they went out to the bars and cafés early and by this time they had gone home to bed.

One idea was that they should go to Kalamaki; there they would certainly find others of the gang, those who went there every night to gawp at the bike freaks. Another group, they knew, had gone down to the night-clubs along the shore. They were fans of Kokkotas, Dionysiou and Marinella* whose songs spoke straight to the dogs' hearts and whose voices earned the general approval of the company. But those who had gone early would have got the best places; and apart from this, they were so devoted to the music that you couldn't have any conversation with them.

A third solution was to go to the airport and watch the planes. As they discussed this and talked of the air-port area they remembered old Fondas who lived over there. How could we have forgotten him for so long! The truth: he had become a bit of a bore; he was on the downhill slope, he had become hopelessly senile said those who had last brought them news of him. But he was their teacher and they loved him. He used to repeat himself, of course. He talked in a murmur; being deaf, he was unable to realize that his voice was getting quieter and quieter, with the result that many of his pupils and friends used to drop off to sleep quickly. But considering that he was said to be nearly eighteen, he wasn't

* Greek popular singers.

in too bad shape. Whole generations had passed through his hands; many of his pupils had long since died a natural death. Old Fondas was now a sort of living legend. He called himself "the Master" and described his school – where complete freedom reigned – as peripatetic. In recent years he had withdrawn to the small kennel in the yard of his former masters' house; they had died years ago and had left the house and land to the State. But since it was so near the airport the house had remained uninhabited and the garden had run wild. Old Fondas haunted the place. At first he used to go in and out of all the rooms and slept wherever he wished. Later, when moving around got difficult for him as his health deteriorated, he used to live in his old kennel in the summer and in winter moved back to the kitchen on the ground floor. This was also something which added to his prestige and to the respect which everyone showed him. When his intellectual powers were at their height, many dogs would find a welcome with him, peace and quiet to sleep, a sheltered place where their wounds could heal, every comfort in which to give birth to their litters.

However, as time passed, it was not only old Fondas who began to disintegrate but also the house. The windows gaped, the doors hung on their hinges and then fell off; in the earthquake of 1981 the roof had collapsed onto the floor of the first storey, then both roof and floor fell onto the floor below. Of course this didn't mean that the house was not still usable by the company. Many of them, though, either because they considered it dangerous or because they were tired of the Master, stopped going there. The kennel in the yard had of course remained intact.

"We should take him something. We can hardly go like this, empty-handed," said Mitsos.

"Like what?" they wondered.

"Keep your eyes open as we go. We'll find something."

They went off with their tails held high. It was a long way to go, but they knew a short-cut from the Wireless which would save them a lot of walking.

Sometimes running and sometimes stopping for a rest they passed through neighbourhoods, they passed wasteland, they passed roads, squares, streams and at last they reached their destination. They used their sense of orientation to find the house; for since old Fondas had stopped going out some time ago, their sense of smell wasn't any help.

Through the transparent evening sky the airplanes were coming down to land like great birds. Their lights were playing on either side, green and red; their headlamps were like rivers of countless tiny night insects or like the frozen breath of animals in winter.

The ruin was still standing about a hundred metres away. They crossed this distance at a run, calling out happily to warn their old friend that they were coming. Cosmas was carrying the piece of soggy bread wrapped in grease-proof paper – which was the only titbit that they had found along the way, but, since the Master couldn't have many teeth left in his mouth, they thought their gift would be welcome.

There was silence from the kennel. Might he be away? Might he have dropped dead? For a moment they thought they saw a shadow. The scent, though, was still there. They went in further. The old dog was asleep. His feeble rattling breathing could be heard in the total silence.

"Luckily," said Thodoras. "As we were coming here I suddenly got the idea that we might not find him."

"Me too," confessed Cosmas. "As soon as I'd suggested visiting him I got second thoughts. It's been such a long time. You never know, do you, what might have happened. I said to myself, haven't we learnt by now?"

They stood there, undecided. The scent reaching them from the kennel was somehow different, they could tell.

"It looks to me as if we've got here just in time," growled Cosmas. "What do you think? Shall we wake him? He mustn't think that we've forgotten him."

"Master!" called Thodoras.

"What are you thinking of, Thodoras?" said Mitsos. "He can't even hear the airplanes now. We'll never wake him by speaking to him. I'll give him a nudge."

They noticed then that old Fondas was sleeping with his nose inside the kennel and his tail outwards. Mitsos went up to his face carefully and gave a gentle nudge to the sleeper's spine. A few moments passed. Mitsos nudged him again. The rhythm of the old dog's breathing altered, a sign that he had woken up. He coughed, then, muttering something incomprehensible, began to back out of his kennel. In the darkness they could make out his familiar face with its drooping ears, its soft lips covering his bare gums, his huge body which his legs could no longer support.

"Who is it?" he asked in a tremulous whine.

He tried in vain to make them out. One by one the gang went up close so that he could identify them by their noses. They had to get right up against old Fondas's nostrils, which were dry and had lost all ability to recognize.

Reassured to recognize his friends, he sank back down on his belly with a happy smile. His voice was so hoarse that it might have belonged to another dog.

"So you remembered me ... and I was thinking, that Nondas...."

"Thodoras, Master."

"Thodoras? Ah, oh yes.... And that Nicos...."

"Mitsos, Master."

"Mitsos, yes. And you, young man, who are you?" the old fellow asked Cosmas.

"I'm Cosmas, Master, don't you remember me? Little Cosmas, the son of Kanella the hunting bitch...."

"I remember Kanella," said the old dog to himself. "She was a good girl. It's been a long time. How did you remember me?"

"Well," said Mitsos, a little embarrassed, "we were just passing and...."

"We thought it was time we came to see you," amended Thodoras decisively.

Old Fondas did not seem to have heard either of them. He coughed once more.

"I'm cold," he said, "cold, in summer! That's why I lie with my nose facing inwards. It's a bad sign, that...."

"It doesn't mean anything," said Cosmas.

"Who is it?"

"I said, it doesn't mean anything! We're cold and we're a whole lot younger.... It's cold in the evenings in the country."

"Yes," said old Fondas, "it's nothing. It's good for a dog to go to his rest.... I'm tired. It's a dog's life, you know what I mean?" he asked Thodoras.

"Why, Master?"

"Loneliness, my boy. All the old ones went such a

long time ago, no one comes to see me now.... And then my legs won't hold me up any more, they won't hold me up. So many years of coming and going.... And I'm not eating any more."

"We've brought something," said Cosmas triumphantly and, picking up the package, he laid it in front of the old dog.

The old teacher bent down and smelled it.

"What is it?" he asked.

The friends looked at each other. There was a lump in their throats.

"It's a piece of soggy bread, Master."

"I can eat that," he mumbled and bent over the grease-proof paper. "Excuse me."

He ate, mumbling his lips and breathing hard in agony; but he left more than half of it and lay down again with his muzzle between his feet. His cloudy eyes looked sad.

"That's it – I've had plenty!" he said. "I can't get any more down.... A few days ago some puppies from round here brought me some bones! Poor things, how could they know? They thought I had something against them because I didn't eat the bones. What could I say? They imagine that everyone has teeth like theirs.... I pant even when I'm lying down – I couldn't even speak to them."

"We could bring something every couple of days," said Cosmas.

"What?"

"I said, we could bring you something to eat every couple of days."

"There's no need," said old Fondas and smiled.

"What do you mean there's no need?" asked Cosmas.

Mitsos trod on his foot lightly.

"There's no need," said the Master. "It seems to me that today or tomorrow I'm going to croak; in fact I'm surprised that I haven't already."

Sadly, the friends lay down in a circle around him. Airplanes were landing and taking off, their noise blotting out the old dog's voice and the utter silence that surrounded his murmur. He was reminiscing about older and younger friends. He began one or two stories and broke off without finishing them; they didn't mind: whatever he said had the magical power to transport them back to their childhoods. At one point he interrupted his incomprehensible stories to ask them if they would come back tomorrow to have a look at him. He would probably be dead. All he wanted was for them to drag him over to that heap of stones, out of the sun and away from the ants' nest. Then he started another half-finished story that all of them had forgotten.

Loved ones came alive again by his words – figures and sometimes familiar scents – forgotten now as if they had never existed. What a world we live in, reflected the friends as they lay, noses between their front legs.

Without realizing it they had grown up. They had left behind them births and deaths, love affairs, friendships that had faded, rows, wars, enmities, persecutions, epidemics which it made them feel sick to remember. And they were now the hunters and the fathers, the husbands and the lovers – yesterday's puppies, still always puppies in the eyes of their Master whose life was now faltering to a close.

They knew that a couple of days after his death they would have forgotten him. Already the planes were drowning his voice, and they could barely make out his shape in the thick darkness of the night. They lifted their eyes, fearful, and saw the deep starry heavens and heard the strange music of the spheres, far away, sometimes threatening, sometimes comforting, always mysterious. The shadows of the trees danced from time to time and crept silently forward over the ground. Under them a whole underworld seethed, invisible, omnivorous – hearing its myriad comings and goings constantly, they became used to it so that they no longer paid any attention.

Was the Master still speaking? Had he stopped speaking? Mitsos got up first to see. He was there in front of them, lying in the same position. The friends looked at each other questioningly, cocked their ears then smelt carefully, each from his own position. The smell that they were receiving now had changed. It had lost the minute movement which resembled the rhythm of respiration; in its place had come a new smell, invisible, motionless, far off, like a visitor standing in the dark.

"We won't need to come tomorrow," muttered Mitsos.

They got up immediately. Thodoras and Cosmas helped him drag the body to the spot which the old dog himself had chosen, beside the heap of stones.

Then, like a guard of honour, they stood round him, raising their muzzles high and intoning a dirge to accompany his soul to its place among the stars of the night. Afterwards, in silence, their tails lowered, they set off back.

"WHO ARE YOU?"

"What do you mean, who am I?" said Petros, "who are you?"

"I'm in my own home," answered the man grudgingly.

"And I'm in your home," said Petros.

"Who is it, Stathis?" came a voice from inside and a woman with an enormous bosom appeared in the hall. "Not any of those fellows who go upstairs, I hope...."

Then, seeing Kouvelas standing there, balding and serious in his embarrassment, she suddenly drew up.

"Doctor, is it you?" she asked. "Let the man in, for goodness sake! What are you standing there for like a block of wood. Move!"

She offered her plump little hand to Petros, her bracelets jingling joyfully.

"Mr. Kouvaras?" she said.

"Kouvelas, yes," said Petros.

"Do forgive us, Mr. Kavouras, we were expecting you!"

"What fellows go upstairs, Madam?" he asked without entering. He had suddenly began to feel very anxious about Minas.

"Why should we speak of them, Doctor, at a time like this, why should we talk of such shameful things?"

Her whole expression had now turned into a mask of affliction. She wrung her fat little hands on her breast which sank like a pillow beneath her black taffeta dress. Her eyes, round as beads, were never still. She had begun to sigh, with the same rhythm as her breathing.

"Come in, Doctor, please excuse us, we're only ignorant people, don't think badly of us!" said Mr. Stathis humbly and closed the door behind him.

"This way ... this way."

The woman went first, clearing the way for them. Kouvelas found himself in a room with seven people, dressed in their Sunday best, sitting round a coffin. The coffin was open and in it lay an old man with an enormous nose like a beak; the green colour of his complexion and this sharp nose made him look like a parrot. Several hands clutched unused handkerchiefs and, apart from a general lack of enthusiasm, the faces did not show any particular grief. They looked more like patients in a waiting room.

"Oh hell," muttered the pseudo-doctor.

Heads turned in his direction. It seems he had spoken aloud. The faces all had something in common: an average Greek family physiognomy, sharp noses, bearing the stamp of similarity with the deceased. Small eyes with bags under them – they reminded one of the eyes of people who've been up all night, except that in this case it was merely one more family characteristic. They couldn't, of course, all be brothers and sisters – but, as people say, after a certain point married couples start to resemble each other. So have Veronica and I started to look like each other then? Probably not; it's too soon. We are still what is called "a youthful couple" or "young people". Young people look like themselves, because each one still looks like his or her parents....

Who are all these dreadful people? And what do they want from me, gathered around their dead relative? You call the doctor when he still might be able to do something, before the inevitable happens. What are they plotting? Who is this doctor that they're all waiting for but that none of them has ever met? How come no one is jumping up and shouting "That's not him!"?

No one moved. They were like an audience watching the entrance of the second actor onto the stage; the first actor being the deceased. Kouvelas, completely unprepared to ad-lib, looked at their faces in case he could pick up any sign as to what he should do. Was it too late to back out? Until the moment that he had entered this funeral chamber everything had been possible. He might, let's say, have found Soulis eating at the family table. Now he was certain that he had made a mistake, that this house couldn't have anything to do with the story. But how on earth does one get out of a funeral chamber? Which was more important now, the superficial or the substantial? He had learnt to make the best of pretences: he hated his work, but had found a way to make it, if not pleasant, at least painless; he suffocated at home, but had found how large a dose of Veronica and the children could be tolerated without them ever turning into his enemies – the opposing camp.

He turned to the couple who had let him in. They had come into the room behind him. The woman was standing near him, while the man called Stathis was pouring a drink from a coloured bottle into a medium sized glass. The pseudo-doctor imagined for a moment that it was going to be offered to him. However, Stathis corked the bottle again and tipped half a glassful straight down his throat.

"Would you like to come next door? The boy's desk is there for you to be more comfortable," said the woman.

He let her lead the way and they went into a small room. There was a desk with high school textbooks and exercise books neatly arranged at one end of the table. The woman pointed to a ballpoint pen.

"Do you need anything else?" she asked him.

"What do you want me to write?" asked Petros.

"I thought that ... I thought that you had agreed on all that with Mr. Adamantiades," the woman said hesitantly. "Surely he told you...."

"He told me, yes. But he didn't give me any details or the particulars of the individual, as we call them; and since I am here with the family of the departed, it would be a good idea if you were to give me them, all of them," he said as coldly as he could, falling back on his professional technique.

"Well, it's about the death certificate," said the woman. "We want it to have today's date ... that's all."

"I know all that," the pseudo-doctor interrupted impatiently. "What I would like you to tell me are the particulars of the departed and the nature of his illness. When did the deceased really die?"

"Two days ago," said the woman sighing, "and that's what makes all the difference. Do you understand now?"

"Naturally, it is extremely important that he should have died today," said Kouvelas.

"You're telling me! It's the difference between day and night," the woman in black laughed jerkily. "The bastard! You'd think he did it on purpose!"

"Indeed," said Petros and heaved a deep sigh.

He sat on the chair in front of the boy's desk.

"And your son, where is he?"

"Soulis! God only knows!" the woman replied, shaking her head in despair. "Ah, Doctor, these children will be the death of us! You never know what company they get mixed up with! And there's nothing you can do, you can't say a word. The boy just gets up and goes off! We lose sight of him for days on end...."

"That's what they are like at that age," said Kouvelas with an air of brooking no objections, trying to swallow the smile which the unexpected discovery had caused to form on his lips.

"How old is he now?" he asked her.

"Our Soulis? Seventeen – the same age as the girl. And he was held back two years running at school! He hasn't got an ounce of brain in his head. He'll be the ruin of us – if you knew the things he gets up to!"

"I've heard something about it," said the pseudo-doctor. "Mad about motorbikes, isn't he?"

The woman looked at him anxiously.

"It's natural at that age. Motorcycles are an affordable means of transport and a good way of showing off; and if they're stolen, the daring of it just adds to the charm!"

"Ah, no! Not stolen, he doesn't steal ... not our Soulis, anyway."

"Of course not," said Petros and preferred to put an end to the discussion. "So what did he die of, the deceased?"

"What do you think he died of?" said the woman, "what I'll die of with those damn kids of mine...."

"Where did he have it?"

"In his liver."

"That's why he's that colour," said Petros. "That will help us get over the fact that he's been dead two days. Where are the papers from the hospital?"

The woman left the room to get them. His eye fell on the open window that gave onto the road. It was two steps away – two steps and a scramble. Before he could move the woman returned. She put various papers down beside him. To get her out of the room again he asked for a glass of water. What he had to do was to write out a medical certificate of death. He'd seen registrars' death certificates often enough, but a doctor's certificate? With a certain sureness he wrote on top of the paper in capital letters CERTIFICATE, then underneath the place and date.

The shutters squeaked. A thief? A burglar? His face was youthful.

"You must be Soulis," Petros said at last, "come in."

For a second the other hesitated. Then, he put his leg over the low sill and hauled himself into the room.

"Are you the doctor?"

"Yes, I am."

"Good!" said the boy. "Where's my mother?"

"Gone to get some water."

Soulis started nervously.

"I don't want her to see me. I only came to get something."

"Under the bed," said Petros, "I want you. Just hide now."

Steps in the corridor. With the suppleness of an acrobat the boy hid himself.

"Here's your water, Doctor."

"Tell me, Madam," said Petros after he'd had a sip of water, "who are all those people gathered here?"

"Relatives and friends," whispered the woman. "They had to be told, didn't they? And to come and pray by his body?"

"Does any of them know?"

"What are you talking about! Nobody! Only cousin Lakis – he's the one with the dark glasses, if you noticed."

"I didn't notice. And Soulis? Does he know?"

"Soulis!" said the woman and gave him a strange look. "It was Soulis's idea...."

"Yes, yes, of course. And now leave the papers with me and go. I've got work to do."

Soulis emerged from under the bed. He shook himself thoroughly and winked boldly at Kouvelas.

"So you're in on it!" he said and stood looking at him with his hands on his hips.

"I am," said Petros, "but I don't understand what difference it would make if we said he had died tonight."

"Ah, well you have to be a lawyer to understand it," said the boy with an air. "Inheritance. Got it, Doctor? It's a big matter."

"All right," said Petros. "I won't ask anything else. But I want you afterwards."

"And why so, if you please?"

"About the motorcycle," he said and transfixed the boy with his gaze.

The terror that spread over the boy's face was almost comic – as if he'd seen the devil in disguise in front of him.

"Which ... what!" he stammered. "OK, I saw it in your face. You're a cop, aren't you?"

"No, I'm not a cop. But you'll have to tell me fair and square where it is. You've caused a lot of trouble tonight with what you've done."

"Who are you?" insisted Soulis.

"I'll tell you," said the pseudo-doctor. "First, though, tell me where Betsy is."

"Who's Betsy?"

"The motorcycle I mean."

"Does it have a name?"

"To its owner."

Soulis laughed.

"She's very well taken care of," he said, "better than if she was a girlfriend. That's why he's given her a name. Don't you worry, uncle, about Betsy; she's in good hands – she was lucky!"

Kouvelas felt that he was in a snake pit – and being called "uncle" was not at all to his taste. The part he was playing had been revealed – he ought to get out of here as fast as possible, and find Betsy. Soulis now seemed indifferent.

"Where have you got her, come on, tell me!"

"What's in it for me if I tell you?"

"I won't hand you over to the police. That's worth something, isn't it?"

"What if I start to scream? Do you know what will happen if those jackals in there find out that you're not a real doctor? Do you know how much money they stand to lose? Do you realize that cousin Koumbatsos always carries a .22 on him to get rid of anyone who's in his way?"

"I can see that you watch a great many films."

"Reality," said Soulis, "is a lot worse."

THE INTERROGATION SEEMED TO LAMBRINOS to have been going on for a century. A sergeant who spoke Greek with a very correct accent had searched his things and asked the stupidest questions imaginable. Two military policemen with fists like sheep hams were guarding the door.

His particulars. Although he had Lambrinos's identity card in front of him, the sergeant seemed to have decided to hear him give his name and details himself, as if he suspected that the identity card might be stolen, forged or altered. Stelios spat out his name and address. As far as his profession was concerned, however, there seemed to be total disbelief on the part of the sergeant –

this was quite clear from the smile that he allowed to flit across his face. WhatarespectableprofessionIchosetogowhoringafter – thought Stelios. They think they know about lawyers! Well dressed, close shaved, pillars of society.... They've never seen our lot from close to.

When it came to how and why he was at the Wireless that evening, things got hopelessly confused. The sergeant could not understand what legitimate rather than suspicious business Lambrinos "and his accomplices" could have had. Moreover, no one else had been discovered around there. Who were his accomplices? What were they called? What did they do.... Lawyers too! And what business did three lawyers have at the radio station at night? We are looking for Betsy, Stelios had said. Who is Betsy; what does she do; how old is she? Betsy is Minas's motorcycle. The sergeant checked his notes, wrote down the new information and looked at him: sometimes frowning, sometimes smiling, sometimes threatening – like a true sergeant. And then, once more, to the radio station. They were looking for Betsy? But he had just said that Betsy was a motorcycle. What was the motorcycle doing by the radio station. What sort of motorcycle was Betsy. Motorcycle ... motorcycle. The kind that you ride; they had been told that the person who stole her was to be found near the Wireless. The sergeant smiled ironically. I shit on you, you bastard, thought Lambrinos. Smile if you like. I, however, am hungry. Emotions make your stomach empty, says Kouvelas.

Then once again a search of his bag. His things spread out on the table under a light, so that no minutest detail should be lost. The magnifying glass – very suspicious. Swallowing the rumbling of his stomach,

Stelios explained with the patience of Job. The glass was for reading.

"What do you read with it? Microfilm?"

"The football pools," said Lambrinos sarcastically.

One of the military policemen growled.

Better not be humorous, thought the prisoner. One more time and they'll throw me to the dogs.

"Why are your eyes wandering like that? Why are you sweating? Are you scared of anything?"

Goddamnyoudirtysonofabitch. Stelios took a deep breath.

"My eyes wander because I don't see very well, I had five operations when I was a child.... I'm sweating because I always do, I sweat very easily."

"A magnifying glass for reading," said the sergeant without expression, and he pushed it aside as if that had been sorted out.

"Yes," said Stelios, "and that over there's a comb. And this is Yellow Fellow, my lighter. Shall I tell you his story? In the spring we went to the village for Easter – it's a village just outside Karpenissi. I was with my young cousin Kimon, the rocker. And all the old folk were there, uncles, aunts, first cousins, second cousins and all the rest of them, everyone had got together. And when the priest says, 'Come take the Light' and the old women take light from him first and everyone lights his candle from the next person's – we light ours and go outside into the courtyard and follow the service from there with our lighted candles, and suddenly puff! a gust of north wind blows them out. Aieee! groan the old women, the Light has gone out and now what will happen since people only want the Holy Light that has been lit from the priest's candle and not from anyone whose candle has blown out right at the beginning? As we were standing a bit higher up, I said that we younger ones – little Kimon and yours truly – would have to go and bring back the Light to the old women. Kimon started cursing and blaspheming against the Resurrection, and on the way I got my lighter out of my trouser pocket and I lit my candle first. 'Come and take the Light', I said to Kimon and I lit his candle. Back we went to the old women, full of joy. 'Did you get it from the priest?' asked Aunt Kontakena who is pretty quick on the uptake. Of course! we say, from the yellow fellow. 'Which one? Which priest?' asks the old woman. 'That one, dear. That one with the red hair and the yellow robe,' says Kimon. What a joooke! And that's how Yellow Fellow stayed with me and I call him Yellow Fellow...."

The sergeant didn't appear to be listening. At the next object he also stopped with great attention. He picked it up with a slow, ritualistic movement and held it in front of the prisoner's eyes for him to identify.

"That's my moustache," said Stelios. "I only wear it at the office. It gives the note of seriousness that befits our distinguished clientèle and adds at least five years to my age, which is very important for a lawyer."

"A false moustache," said the sergeant expressionlessly and noted it down in his notebook. "A means of disguise."

"Let's just call it a professional secret," suggested Stelios in a spirit of compromise.

"Do you take us for fools?" asked the sergeant.

"I'm hungry," said Stelios. "Why don't we break off for you to fetch a hot dog or some doughnuts or something?"

"A notepad with telephone numbers," said the

sergeant, putting this too on one side.

"Girlfriends," explained Stelios.

"What about this little jar?" said the other, unscrewing it and sniffing the contents.

"Explosives, what else? Come on, it's vaseline.... You know, to stop my hands from cracking."

The sergeant looked at him mistrustfully.

"You lean forward and I'll whisper in your ear what I use it for," said Stelios coyly.

"I'll ram it down your throat," threatened the other.

The search continued. A knife blade. A compass.

"So I don't get lost at night."

"But tonight you got lost."

"That was because I couldn't find the compass."

There was an old broken key ring, bought from old Yannakos's kiosk in Batané Square. How could you explain things to this ox; the more he told him, the more he felt that he was making a worse and worse impression.

Finally, the book. The little book. "Comrade Leon, you've torn it!" thought Stelios. "I'll really have to learn to return borrowed books."

"Call the major!" said the sergeant in English to one of the military policemen. The book seemed to have been the last straw; his stock as a spy had risen dizzyingly.

With the calm movements of a man of routine, the sergeant opened a cupboard against the wall, a metal door with screws which as it opened revealed some kind of console with buttons and graded dials with indicators and little lights. A switch put the strange machine into action: the lights came on, and the dials lit up without any mechanical sound. From another cupboard beside the console he took a sort of crane, an angled metal frame from the top of which hung threads and electrodes.

"Get him ready," said the sergeant to the remaining military policeman, and the latter came up to the prisoner.

"Can you grill chops on that machine, boys," asked Stelios, in whom hunger was vying with fear so that, to tell the truth, he didn't know which of the two was weighing more heavily on his stomach.

The policeman immobilized him against the back of the chair, passing a strap around his chest, and tying his arms to his sides. Quick as lightning he tied his lower legs together. Stelios screamed and began to curse and swear. A hood was passed over his head and everything went dark. He could breathe, though; this was some consolation. He could continue talking and swearing non-stop – though for the time being this didn't seem quite possible, since, straining his attention, he was making a vast effort to be aware of what was going on round him, all the nerves in his whole body waiting for the attack, the pain.

Footsteps in the corridor. The door. Someone came in, someone went up to the console behind him, someone else suddenly was standing at the table with the contents of his bag strewn over it. They were speaking English, with that nauseating American accent that seems to touch every vowel in the language with hate and hostility. Something like a metal crown, not tight-fitting, was placed over his head.

"We are ready, Dr. Melis," he heard the voice which must have been the major's say.

"Everything set up," said a voice beside the console.

"Have a nicey-nice timey," thought Stelios.

"Let's go."
"He says he is called Stylianos Lambrinos, a Greek subject, profession lawyer, resident of Athens, Batané Square," he heard the sergeant's voice as if he was reading the notes he had taken from his notebook.
"I am whatever I like," thought the prisoner "and a lawyer and I shit on wanking cowherds like you."
"He denies that he is or ever was a member of any organization opposed to or fighting against the policy of the government of the United States of America," continued the sergeant to his invisible audience.
"I'd answer, pal, if I had a fart ready," Lambrinos gritted his teeth. "Look what I've gone and got myself into! Dear, dear! This is some sort of machine, I've read about it in the newspaper: a lie detector or whatever they call it.... And my friends are waiting for old Lambrinos's help! And like a goat I got my head down and set off and listened to directions from various odd bodies till I managed to get myself to the radio base at Nea Pangri! And as if all that wasn't enough, I'm taken prisoner with my little jar of vaseline and that fucking book of Leon Davidovitch with the picture of the author large and clear on the front cover so that there shouldn't be any doubt about it."
He felt crushed: he had certainly let down his friends who needed him, he'd made a fool of himself, he'd got himself into trouble again by his old weakness – suddenly all the feelings of painful isolation that he had experienced as a child were awoken once more from the forgotten place where the passing years had buried them, the slow and painful rehabilitation that he had achieved through hard effort. The checking of his political persuasions was complicated by the damned book

which he had been carrying around, for months now, in his bag. He'd borrowed it from his Freak Olia who had introduced him to his other two Freaks, Christinaki and Errikoula, in order to make a good impression on them, that he was the sort of person who read books and so on, an intellectual and a revolutionary and an anarchist – for how else could a lawyer get to fuck a Freak? The only bit that he'd read in all this time was the first twenty pages – then he always fell asleep, whether or not he was tired.... "But, you creeps, we have every right to have any book we like in our bag. In any case I'm master of my own little mindy and I don't care too muchy for your gynaecologist's chair! And I'm called Stelios and Master Stelios.... Dig it!"

"He denies that he came to Nea Pangri with the intention of penetrating the prohibited zone together with a group of friends of similar persuasions with the purpose of committing acts of sabotage and/or explosive activities."

"How much do people get paid for making such amazing discoveries?" wondered the prisoner furiously. "Hedeniesityousaiditpal! What he wouldn't say no to would be a good joint of meat – that's as certain as that you are a whole lot stupider than I thought. As for penetrating into prohibited zones, what I have in mind is of a quite different kind.... I always fancied it, as they say, like a true bon viveur, a Turkish hedonist, as well as other related pleasures (Aaah! Penny) of a cunnilingual nature, washed down with a beer and a roast chicken from 'Alekos's' and to finish off a double kataifi like the ones my dear departed late godmother used to make, God have mercy on her soul, drenched in cherry syrup or a seven-layer baclava with white almonds and rose water. And while we're putting things in terms of appetite, what I need right now to restore me is a double helping of Salonica gyro and lashings of finely chopped onion and parsley and two spoonfuls of mustard, really hot; pitta bread grilled in fat and plenty of red pepper.... And to quench the fire of all these explosive ingredients two bottles of beer – whatever brand you've got, but chilled! To be chewed rapidly and greedily – for that's how these things should be eaten.... I don't rule out a bit of country-style stuffed meat or sausage, if my appetite can take it and my stomach still has any room left.... To follow, the body should be in a slightly reclining position so as not to put pressure on the lungs.... And then, after this, a phone call to the Freaks – who arrive promptly; (the Freaks are the best choice since the meal contained so much onion and garlic – for the Freaks aren't put off by such details; quite apart from the fact that Christinaki and Errikoula, for ideological reasons and as a reaction to our enslavement to deodorants, allow their bodily odours free reign... and it's a real feast of the senses, Sergeant, to smell their little feet and their little arses, as these are laid bare....). Of course, these are not standard everyday pleasures – you need a special proclivity, talent and maturity..... If you tell Minas about odours he is capable of abstaining for a whole week.... I've always said it: people don't seem to love the body. In the last analysis they do all they can to separate sexual functions from the body and then struggle to get any pleasure without it. The world and sex, as the Old Man used to say, belong to the bon viveurs. Dig it!"

"Professor Melis! The detector has broken down!" said the major, with a touch of schadenfreude in his voice.

"WHERE'S THIS ROAD TAKING US?" wondered Kouvelas.

The rocker sitting beside him in Lulu gives directions "turn here – turn there". All this muddle seems to him to be pointless and false, all this sudden familiarity with someone he didn't know and would never have expected to know. Soulis himself, however, appears to find it all entirely natural: nothing in his behaviour shows any surprise – no surprise that something, however you look at it, is taking place which doesn't occur every day in his raw schoolboy's life; no surprise at becoming familiar with someone like Kouvelas, with a successful lawyer for whom half the secrets of Piraeus are an open book, with an adult; for we're the adults now, our year at school now hold all the important positions, we bring up children, we teach students, we drive around in cars like Lulu (the sedan snorted with pleasure), we keep mistresses.... And if we were ambitious we'd have positions in public life, a principal secretaryship here, a junior ministerial seat there, and who knows what.... And the rocker beside me says this way, that way, turn there, and I turn. And he's worth stealing a glance at, this little bird. And he smells sweet.

"Nice car you've got," said Soulis.

"Like it?"

Out of the corner of his eye he saw that the boy was looking at him from his seat.

"Where are we going?" he asked neutrally; he had already asked this question and always got the same response; the rocker was acting mysterious.

"You'll see."

Something in the communication between them – when they spoke, that is – didn't seem to be working quite right. Petros's words and expressions seemed to take on another meaning in Soulis's ears; and it was as if he hadn't heard him at all or as if he couldn't penetrate their obscure meaning. And the language the boy spoke was something else again! He could understand the words one by one – he'd heard them before. But the sentences that they formed had something utterly Sibyllic about them – like the Megairan oracle.

It's impossible for me to love you, thought Petros, without understanding himself what he meant. It had become quite clear in the last few minutes that the boy was taking him towards Piraeus.

"Why did you steal the bike, come to that?"

"Why have you got such a nice car?"

He's a bit of everything all mixed up; a touch of the anarchist, a touch of the teddy boy, a touch of the lad – and he's got beautiful hands. So what do you mean by letting yourself get dragged so far from the bastard's house? And Minas? Is he still there? Has he left? Where's he got to? Since Petros had found Soulis, where could Minas have got to? The enterprise was supposed to be a common one.... The general lost, Minas lost, Stelios lost, old man Restis lost, Betsy lost, Piraeus lost (would he be able to find his way where they were going?), everything lost.

Just after a turning he recognized the road. He realized, amazed, that it was the road that he took every morning, on his way to the office in Lulu. Just think, how much we don't know.... This road was something so well-known and habitual – he used to drive down it on automatic pilot to give himself a bit more time to daydream, to think about the work awaiting him, the phone calls, the meetings – that the thought had never crossed his mind that it might also exist in parallel as another different, narrower road, other houses and other corners watching him go by every morning at the same time.

Petros launched himself into this explosion of his benumbed brain beyond the everyday, certain that he was thinking new and extremely significant thoughts – his hairs were already standing on end with the shiver of creativity. We ought to be able to think more often – to devote more time in the day to contemplation: just see what the mind discovers when you let it go off the leash a little. However, it's not the right moment to let yourself go now. Where's this young layabout beside you taking you – have you wondered? I've wondered, but I haven't got anywhere.

"Are the girls in your class good looking?" he asked the boy.

The boy gave a smothered laugh.

"Ace."

"Do they like it?"

"They like it. You keep your word. You're OK, you are. Would you like to meet one?"

"Two," said Kouvelas.

This was something that he had been coming to have more and more of a taste for recently. If he'd had his sons ten years earlier, like others of his contemporaries had done, he would have been able to count on the girls in their classes. All kept secret from Veronica, of course, secret. It used not to be like this. My life has become full of secrets – I've heard that somewhere, but where.... When we were younger our lives were an open book, we wanted everyone to be able to bend down and read it –

so that we would be loved (the eternal goal!). Now we keep the book under heavy seals – once again so that we'll be loved.... By people. What people? Is Soulis people? So that Soulis will love me – what am I doing? His beautiful long willowy fingers are playing on his knee. What does he think of you? That you are one of them, the grown-ups who rule the world and set the rules which it is so sweet for him and the girls who fancy him to break.... That you stay unbudging and unmoved, a wall for dogs to piss on, a building for Soulis to go in and out of, to live in, a road for people to walk on.... Something like that. He feels he has the right to drag you through the streets of Piraeus at night and not to bother to make himself comprehensible when he speaks to you – like he would in front of the first policeman he might come across or cousin Koumbatsos with his .22 in his pocket.

"Turn left," said Soulis as soon as they passed the clock. "And I've got some beautiful classmates."

Kouvelas felt a pain in his stomach. He answered with a groan – though not a discouraging one. Does it really matter? The same night covers Mairoula or Vipsy – the same night covers Soulis – one secret more to be locked in the casket ... and the casket cast on the waves – at the end of the play – for future generations to find it and never learn a thing.

Betsy couldn't be very far off. Or the office either – or the bachelor flat, come to that, which most conveniently was in the street parallel. They had taken a narrow road which led down to the central harbour of Piraeus from Pashalimani. The blinds were down over shops; a chemist with a light over the card showing which chemists were on duty that night. Rubbish piled in heaps at the entrances of apartment buildings. The street lamps hanging from building to building on metal loops. Little trees waiting in vain for the water lorry of the Municipality to water them.

Soulis – who knows Soulis or pays any heed to him. He could never belong to the category of people whose opinion matters. A bit of an anarchist, a bit of a thug, a bit of a lover boy. A young and silly kid who thinks he can drive the bus from the bar on the front seat. The fewest words, the simplest and slightest pretext would be enough for him. For example, you could say, "Shall we go upstairs for a minute and have a drink?" You say it and it's a relief. The young are like flowing water. They shift easily, from one mood to another, from one role to another – since the boundless possibilities, the boundless perspectives, the boundless shades of all roles, all of which move them equally, can each time transform their faces, their behaviour, their voices into something totally different. In the mists of his imagination he could glimpse the harmonious body, shapely, supple, he could see the boy's eyelids drop modestly veiling his eyes, the smile familiar from paintings by Da Vinci. Betsy's bold kidnapper could in an instant become a tender dependent, could pass as if enchanted into that kind of pre-erotic mood, common to both the sexes, as each turns towards the other. His own movements would aquire a different weight. Putting the key in the door would mean something more, turning on the light, pulling up the blinds at the window, to let a little fresh sea air in through their slats. Walking over to the lamp, or opening the door of the fridge which squeaked absurdly – such ordinary everyday movements would be transformed into parts of a ritual, would be full of symbolism and hopes. There were a mass of named and nameless presences here which had left their faded scent all around, a fluttering host whose traces remained imprinted like shadows on the walls, on the furniture, in the atmosphere of the small flat; they would quiver faintly as they tried to awaken, to arise and to inhabit once more the place which they had forever abandoned. "Ghosts, ghosts everywhere ... and regrets, regrets for approaches which had been frozen at a particular moment of time like photographs, motionless, fixed, incapable of advancing further, of evolving, of developing their power and their potential – unnaturally arrested in the poses which were what our conventions demanded, their conventions demanded, predetermined by the roles which we allot to others and others allot to us. Perhaps it's better this way...."

MINAS HAD NEVER EXPECTED that this ugly girl would be something so special. As if a veil had been drawn from before his eyes, he recognized something ideal, unsuspected, in her strange features – as sometimes happened with food that he didn't eat often and was sure he didn't like, then suddenly discovered how delicious it was.

In the expressions of her small face was distilled all the magic of erotic love. Her childlike body could dominate him, could awaken in him a desire which it seemed nothing could quench – except her body itself. At the beginning he thought that this magic was due to the fact that he had been honest with her. But then what relation to anything did the idiotic story he had told her bear? Was it not possible that the truth was nothing more for Gia than another layer of lies? Why this and not that? Something different had happened.

She had pulled her shirt over her head; from it her small dark head peeped out a little comically, as if out of a bag; she was naked, revealing to his dazzled eyes a perfect body, a beauty that was painful to him. Before Minas could form from within himself one of those phrases that he used to employ in order to frame circumstances, Gia came and lay down on top of him, and led him into a secret garden whose existence he had never suspected, to which only she held the key, whose secret paths she alone knew.

He had the impression that she was his true love, whom he was finding once more, and that Evanthitsa was one of those transient adventures, so-called casual encounters, like Vipsy at the office or Stelios's Freaks. She seemed to be the answer to the dreams he had dreamed as he watched girls in the street; she was like something which had begun long ago, which some happy awakening of the senses had at last made him able to notice and to appreciate.

From the bedroom window came the scent of jasmine and, far off, the howling of mourning dogs. Their bodies, anointed with the sweat of their struggle, touched and parted and came together again; their breath was sweet; their fingers wandered ceaselessly over the gentle hills of the human landscape. He tried hard to see her eyes; but most of the time the girl had her eyelids lowered, with something like modesty, with something of a musician's concentration as he plays; she seemed to move with sureness, like that of the blind in the environment that they know best. A blush spread over her face, her knitted eyebrows bearing witness to her infinite devotion to the act taking place. She was like the Pythia, strengthened through sacred intoxication until at last she is able to recognize the truth and utter the oracle. "An Athenian mistress – the best there is!" She was moaning rhythmically, now with her mouth open and now with her lips clenched tight in a grimace of pain. And he, sometimes thrown beneath the girl like a hammer which will be struck from on high by the anvil, sometimes flowing over her like a parachutist in free fall, sometimes curved by her side like her twin crescent moon, tried to absorb as much as he could of this miracle which he feared might never be repeated.

What had just happened was a flight over the world, with Gia in place of Betsy – the same feeling of conjunction, of their union into one being, like the mythical centaur whose two parts maintain their separate shape but are joined by invisible nerves, the one emptying into the other like twin mirror images. It was something which until that night Minas had not known could exist in love.

Gia nested close in his arms; the record had finished playing for the second time and was ready to start again. The Rolling Stones, just like back then. And Momos, the snake, waiting patiently and looking at him from the floor where he had been hurled during their struggle. Suddenly everything was over and Evanthitsa, his friends, Betsy, the general were all waiting for him to return to them, to help, to take part, to do something which would provide a solution and an end to tonight's adventure. He had finished, it was the end. The girl got up from beside him, went to the window and looked out. Then she went out of the room. He heard water running. Then he saw her again in the doorway, naked like an invitation, a promise that everything could start again, happen again, reoccur. Evanthitsa used to return wrapped in a towel like a toy ready to be put back in its box. She lit a cigarette and placed it in his mouth.

"How did you know?" asked Minas.

"All men smoke afterwards," said Gia.

Minas got up. His clothes were strewn over the floor in approximately the right order for putting them on again.... Once more: his friends, Betsy, Evanthitsa, his uncle and his father.

"And do they all want to see you again afterwards?" he asked looking at her.

Gia did not say anything. She was thinking.

"No," she said finally. "Why should they want to? It all stops about here, doesn't it? We reached the end at once."

He wanted to tell her.... Thousands of words flooded his mind, he felt that he was drowning in them. He wanted to protest, to talk to her of beginnings, of new starts, of dates, of phone calls, of fires which once lit spread and burn down whole areas.... But as soon as they reached the tip of his tongue he was ashamed to say them, so unsuitable and cheap and easy did they seem. "But it can't be too difficult if I really want it," he thought. "She doesn't seem to be pushing me out, nor does she seem to have regretted it – anything but! She is just putting on her little act, like they all do afterwards."

He got dressed. The girl was still naked, sitting cross-legged on the mattress.

"I'll come back tomorrow," he told her. "I'll take you out."

Gia put on her shirt.

"No," she said. "Look: tomorrow my brother will have sorted things out with your motorbike. He doesn't do any damage to motorbikes. They just give him a kick. He takes them to ride around on a bit. He always returns them. He will probably have left it outside your house already. He hasn't really got his feet on the ground; he wants to live better than he really can. It isn't good, but it isn't a crime – it's natural."

"Nothing is a crime if it means that I met you," said Minas.

She pouted mockingly. "Big words!" a critical voice within him said. So what would she like? What would move her?

"I don't care about the bike," he said. "I've forgotten it already. Like it had never existed. I could sell it to Soulis if he wanted.... And if he hasn't got enough money, he could pay me in instalments...."

"Why d'you buy it, then?"

"I liked it," said Minas emotionally. "The way I liked my girlfriend till today. From today I only like you...."

"You like yourself," said Gia. Her face dissolved in a childlike impish smile but she was still speaking seriously. "It shows," she said.

"How does it show?"

She was silent and had turned her eyes to the floor once more. She didn't seem willing to answer. And Minas felt wounded, belittled. How could she presume to judge him? How could she judge him, when she had no idea what he was like, what his world was like? He insisted, asking her again and again, but Gia continued not to answer. What made her think something like that? How could a kid like her, lost down here behind the Wireless, make diagnoses? And why did she remain as much of an unsolved mystery to him after making love as she was before? Was it because he had kept his eyes open throughout? But how could he have stopped looking at such a miracle, even for a moment? Had she understood the flood of worry and angst which had arisen in him as soon as they had finished? Was it possible that in his eyes she had seen the reflections of all the people and things that he carried about with him and that he felt were calling him back to them? Could she have recognized something about him from the fine words that he liked to use? The girl didn't explain.

Minas got up.

"I've got to go," he said.

"Shall I turn on the light on the stairs for you?" Gia asked. Just as if she was already erasing everything with a damp sponge.

"No, there's no need, I can see."

He went out into the corridor alone, reached the hall, stood in front of the door. Then he noticed the telephone on the shelf of the strange sofa. He lifted the receiver and memorized the number that was written on the little label beneath it.

"Happy queens and joyful gays
prance along in queerish bliss,
singing through the nights and days,
stopping only for a kiss"

The song poured forth from six throats, cheerful and provocative. The company were all drunk. On his arm the general had the retired solicitor who was known in these circles as Bebeka or Boubou. Behind them came the rest of the company, all of them around the same age as the general, short in stature, dressed in casual slacks with their shirts unbuttoned, revealing all manner of baubles hanging round their necks, beads and crosses and chains. Four of them were walking behind Bebeka and the general and were singing their own strange words to a well-known tune with all their might.*

Behind the human company came the dog company, which now included (they had met by chance on the way) Menios, Vangelitsa, Fouskas, Trelaras and Maniatissa – five more mongrels. During the greetings and the friendly teasing, Cosmas remembered and told them about the death of old Fondas. They shook their heads sadly, but a few steps further on they had already forgotten. Still a bit upset and frightened by the smell of death, Cosmas screwed Vangelitsa and Thodoras Maniatissa – although usually they didn't fancy them all that much. Then, as they made their way all together down towards Piraeus, they had come across the company of old men and had followed them at a distance. Both groups were going in the same direction, but the old men didn't quite seem to have decided how far they were going together. They were walking slowly, out of step, and every so often one of them would stop and begin to recount some hilarious story. Then, laughing, they'd move on again.

The general was completely sober. He had run into Bebeka while he was trying to get information about Soulis. He knew that the solicitor, since he had – recently – become a widower, was throwing all his

* In the original text the words to the song and the conversation between the general and Bebeka are in *kaliarda*, the Greek homosexual dialect.

money away on boys; the general was sure, for many reasons, that it was he who had spoiled his affair. Like a lover who attempts to make contact again with his former mistress, he was trying to fish for information; however, the solicitor was either too drunk to make sense or else was not drunk at all and was baiting the general, knowing how emotional he was and how much love affairs cost him.

It was late and the stars were high in the sky, moving over to the west. In the peace of the coast road, broken only by passing cars, came the sound of the gentle waves, breaking and dying on the pebbles of the beach. They had passed the Hippodrome and were walking along past the last houses of Kallithea.

Salmo the Blanket had thrown into the general confusion the idea of perhaps going to meet some pilots behind the changing rooms of the Karaiskaki Stadium. The company was tipsy and had taken the road in that direction, gossiping and singing. In the darkness that reigned they looked like a troupe of ghosts as they kept stopping short then starting again, drawing apart then moving on together again. Their song came and went, and the blackness of the night absorbed their weak, womanly-thin voices like blotting paper.

> *"... singing through the nights and days,*
> *stopping only for a kiss"*

"Beba," said the general seriously, "if you tell me one secret I'll tell you another. Your secret will save me a lot of trouble tonight, and when it comes down to it, that little snot can't go on acting clever – it's Soulis I'm talking about! He's nicked a motorcycle of ours and I've been looking for him all evening. Just tell me where he's hanging out and he'll escape the long arm of the law. I'm telling you, it's serious. He's exposed me to my family.... And I've got a secret for you straight from the top which you'll forget immediately you've heard it. I'm saving your life, baby, right now today, you'll see, it's not just any old teeny weeny little favour that I'm doing you...."

The old solicitor realized that the general was serious and he sobered up at once.

"I know you quite well, René," he said.

The general was known as Rena or René because of his royalist tendencies, which it seemed had had something to do with his early retirement from the army.

"You're not going to tell me about the tanks which I saw going up past Syntagma Square yesterday?"

"Yes, I am, just that...."

"Which means?"

"Just what you imagine, you clever little girl. Yes.... I shall be one of the top brass. And the green berets will soon be getting a look at me at some of their weekly briefings at headquarters. And at that point, our good friends will get all the little favours that they want...."

"Do you mean it seriously?" asked the solicitor. "I've got some young friends that it might be a good idea to warn. This time of year they hang out on the islands...."

"It would be wise if they got their passports in order," recommended the general with utter seriousness.

"Are you talking seriously, René?" asked the solicitor, frozen with fear, as if he had only just taken in the import of what he'd heard.

"Cross my heart!" said the general. "So now, tell me...."

"I don't know all that much," stammered the other. "Not even if the boy's telling lies – but he told me a few days ago that he was smitten with a girl in his neighbourhood.... That's what he said, anyway. Now, whether that's the true reason why he's disappeared from the scene neither I nor anyone else can tell...."

They had stood still as they talked and the rest of the group had passed them and had gone on to the end of the road, while behind them followed the gang.

"I'm not getting anywhere here" thought the general, looking at his watch in despair. "I'd better find a taxi and get back to Iolaos and his young scion. Boubou, if you're having me on," he said, turning once more to the other, "you'll have me to answer to, not God, in a few days' time."

"I'm telling you what he told me...."

From far off the song was heard again. The general looked this way and that along the coast road; the cars were few and far between, you could cross easily without danger. In the end, though, he preferred to go back towards the Delta so as to find a taxi more easily. Without saying goodbye to anyone he turned round and began walking. The solicitor followed him for a while, then began to run back towards the company in order to catch them up before they got any further away.

The general covered the distance separating him from the Hippodrome with a rapid step. The lights of passing cars, coming towards him as they headed for Piraeus, shone on his face: he was pale and drops of sweat were trickling down from his forehead onto his pinched cheeks. He swears to himself that this is the last time he will lose his cool. Old age has caught up with him and he feels as if he has turned utterly to jelly. When he was younger he was fiercer – he could get his way without any effort. Tonight had been a weakness, a moment of terror which had got the better of him. Soulis had said it and had done it – it was his fault for not having believed him. So what was to be done? Should he let the police get mixed up in the case and have the boy start blackmailing him? His eyes flash. He has recovered: reality is never quite as terrifying as fear. There is a very simple explanation for everything. He mustn't delay any more. He must go back to being his own self, must reflect, concentrate, recover what his weakness and lack of will have allowed to slip out. He feels that after a long break the time for action has arrived once more. In a few days' time his cares and preoccupations will be quite different. He will be reborn, he will feel again, everything will once more find its true place; and pleasures will then come in due course to smooth away the fatigue of warriors who fight for their fatherland.

However, Minas mustn't be allowed to keep tonight's picture of him, the Batané Square picture. Soulis must be found and punished – the general's heart has turned to stone once more. As he walks his step becomes firm, decisive, rapid. Everything will soon be sorted out.

Behind the wall of the Hippodrome four dogs are approaching the stables in the happy anticipation of meeting their friends. In the open-air parking lot cars are standing, their interior lights off. The unsuspecting eye would never imagine what is going on inside them. Sodom and Gomorrah. All these worms, thinks the general. All these bestial sodomites, young men who could have stayed where they belonged with their rakes, their hoes, their combine harvesters, and begotten children, so that this many-headed monster of the capital city would not have come into being. In his imagination he hears his voice magnified through a loudspeaker and echoing throughout the whole country. "They arrive here drawn by the voluptuous pleasures of Circe, thinking that life is the way the cinema shows it – and they become slaves, garbage collectors, anything you can think of, they forget God and man's proper place in the land where he was born. And the cinema bears its share of the blame; instead of showing things as they really are, it gives a false picture to the Greek provinces. The pursuit of pleasure and a low birth rate! An entire nation abandons itself to unspeakable orgies, young people go round with drugs and contraceptives, while our enemies are breeding like rabbits: the Bulgarians are only waiting to cross the Haemos and the Turks the Hebrus. Once and for all! The knife! These things cannot be cured except by the surgeon's knife (the scalpel or whatever it's called). I'll be back before long!" promises the general, casting a threatening look backwards at the car park of the Hippodrome. "And then I'll be different.... It's not for nothing that I have learned your secrets, you useless worms.... And even these stray mongrels that roam through the streets uncontrolled, carriers of disease, sources of pollution.... Poison, the dog catcher – and we'll be free of them forever.... The entrance, they call it, to a European capital city – and it is worse than a casbah, worse than the nigger alleys of Cairo."

In the hot summer atmosphere, the radiance of the street lamps on both sides of the road cast a brief halo, blotted up by the night.

The general crossed to the opposite pavement hoping to find a taxi. It took twenty minutes before one stopped.

He was boiling with impatience and irritation. He gave the address to the driver in a clipped military tone. The driver put down the flag.

"And this will change too!" said the general, furious.

"What will change, sir?"

"Not being able to find a taxi at any time of the day!"

"You give us licenses then, and we'll have taxis on the road, why don't you give out more licenses?" answered the driver.

"It's not the licenses that are to blame, it's the whole mentality that will have to change.... Greeks don't understand words. All they need is the whip!"

"Aha, there I agree with you, sir!" replied the taxi driver and from that point on said nothing more to his passenger.

At Koutloumousiou Square an unexpected sight awaited him. Minas was standing beside a stranger, a plump slightly balding gentleman, by a white sedan, and behind the white sedan Iolaos Restis had manoeuvred the general's old cabriolet and was sitting at the wheel with a worried air.

The general cast an eye around. There was not a sign of Soulis; was it possible then for him to feel easy? But he preferred to take Iolaos back to his sister's anyway. The joke had gone on long enough, he himself had not succeeded in anything, other people had got mixed up in the case and it was natural that things should have gone awry. He had to find out, though.

With an abrupt nod in Kouvelas's direction he went up to his nephew and drew him aside. Minas told him the good news. Betsy had been found.

"Did you find her?"

"No, Petros did. He found her near our office. She

was leaning against the lamppost where I usually tie her!"

"And Soulis?"

"Not a trace of him. It looks as if he didn't have anything to do with it."

The general looked at him in disbelief.

"Petros," continued Minas, "in reality suspected the colleagues from the office above ours. They've got an old grudge against us. He says that the idea suddenly came to him. He remembered that when we left this afternoon he saw them watching us from their window upstairs...."

Kouvelas was only too willing to describe his adventure in every detail. Not finding Soulis at the house where he was looking for him and having lost Minas, he went back to the square to get his car. But he couldn't get out of his head the sight of Prokos and Stokos watching them from upstairs as they left that afternoon. ("Let me introduce you," interrupted Minas. "My uncle, General Stefanos Orlovsky...." "Retired; how do you do!" said the general. "My friend and colleague from the office, Petros Kouvelas." "How do you do," said Petros and continued his narrative.) This was something that he had wanted to tell Minas right from the beginning, when he telephoned him and announced the catastrophe. However, something had held him back. Perhaps the certainty that such things couldn't possibly happen between colleagues. Anyway, since there was no one at their agreed rendezvous at the square, he took his car and went down to Piraeus. He went into the office, turned on the lights and went straight to the answering machine. ("Good God, your other friend hasn't turned up yet," said Iolaos Restis from the wheel of the cabriolet. Petros and Minas looked at each other with a smile of complicity. "Hardly surprising if he's driving Marmaro himself!" said Minas. "But let's not interrupt the story.") Every morning the answering machine is switched over to recording once the secretary has noted down the phone calls, and whichever of the friends leaves last turns it on. Kouvelas played the tape back. And, miracle, there were already phone calls. One was from a client. It was Mr. Fokianos who requested Petros to contact him as soon as he got in to the office. The next two were "silent" calls (as Stelios called them, who was driven crazy by people who hung up as soon as they heard the answering machine). But there was a fourth call. An unknown voice had left a very short but significant message. "The motorcycle is in its usual place." Immediately he wondered which its usual place was. Outside Minas's house? He went back down to the street, undecided as to what was best to do. Betsy was leaning against the lamppost, just where her master chained her every day.

"May I have a word with you in private, Counsellor!" said the uncle politely but firmly, as he drew Petros aside. "I don't wish to cast the slightest doubt on what you have told us ... but you must bear in mind that we had different information about the thief. It seems he is an unfortunate boy for whom, so to speak, I am now responsible, through his uncle who is an old friend of mine but who is now seriously ill so that sadly he is unable to manage the affairs of his own household, if you understand what I mean.... He is the boy called Soulis. And I must confess that his whole comportment up to now as well as the specific threats which he has directed against me in the recent past make him very much more to be suspected than your office's competitors who are, moreover, older and are professional gentlemen. Tell me in all truth – and be sure that the young man, whom, without any doubt, you are protecting out of generosity, will not suffer the least consequence.... Whatever you say will remain strictly between ourselves...."

The general's eyes ran over Petros's face without stopping, without missing a single contraction of his features.

"I am interested, as his guardian."

"Did you say that his uncle was gravely ill?"

"Cirrhosis of the liver, to call things by their proper names."

"And his parents?"

"They're rather low sort of people. They have taken my unfortunate friend into their home supposedly to look after him, but in reality they are bleeding him dry and are only after his money – of which he has quite a lot. As far as other things are concerned, they encourage – probably for profit – the ... the tendencies to a dolce vita, let's put it like that, not only of the boy but also of his younger sister. A sad situation ... I don't want to expand on it much more."

"I understand," said Petros. "But what could you, as an outsider, do?"

"A lot! Provided that I know of his actions and am in a position to keep a constant eye on his movements."

Petros remained silent for a moment.

"Soulis's movements," he said after a while.

"Exactly!" said the general.

Soulis's. But not his younger sister's.

"It's really a very fine thing that you're doing, General. Unfortunately ... unfortunately I'm not in a position to make any contribution to your efforts to bring this unlucky boy up right.... No, seriously!" he said, looking his interlocutor in the face, "perhaps it may be a sign for the best – perhaps in the last analysis he may really have no connection with the theft. Maybe someone wanted to slander him to you...."

The general stared at him curiously, with an expression which bore witness to his utter embarrassment.

"Nevertheless, he was seen tonight with Minas's motorcycle," he said, interrupting Petros who was continuing to produce various phrases.

"He was seen? All right. It means that when it comes down to it we can't exclude him," confessed the lawyer. "What you know from your sources is certainly more reliable than what I know. Certainly I would not be in a position, so to speak, to tell you whose voice it was on the answering machine. It could, in the end, have been your protégé's."

"If I heard the tape I would be able to be sure!" said the general with some warmth. "I know that boy's voice extremely well."

"Unfortunately I erased the tape," said Petros coldly.

The general looked at him askance.

"And your telephone number? How could he have known who owned the motorcycle?"

"Since he knows you, I don't see why he shouldn't know your nephew," said Petros and the general paled, his anxious eyes revealing how hard he was thinking and with what rapidity his thoughts were turning over in his mind. "Minas always leaves his motorcycle in the same place every day; and our office is only a few steps away."

The general could do nothing to hide the unnatural flush which had spread over his pale pinched face.

"So ... so you didn't see Soulis at all, you neither," he whispered finally, his eyes on the ground.

"Not at all!" said Petros with the air that he had when he required Veronica to believe his words completely. "One would think, General, that you weren't very pleased about it."

A half smile and a slight shrug of the shoulders were the only answer he received. The uncle went back over to Iolaos Restis.

"Time for us to go! Your mother will be getting worried, Minas."

"Are you sure, boys, that you will be able to manage by yourselves?" asked old Restis.

They reassured him. Elders and youngers bade farewell to each other with elaborate politeness.

"Until we meet again, young gentlemen!" called Uncle Stefanos from the car.

AS SOON AS THEY HAD DISAPPEARED round the corner, Minas stormed Kouvelas like someone whose elders' presence had until now prevented him from saying all that he wanted. He was shining bright as the sun.

"Where have you got her? Where is she?"

"She's at the Mobil station at Pashalimani" said Petros. "Don't worry. It's open all night. No matter what time we go they'll give her to us. Anyway, I told them about what had happened...."

"I've got something to tell you as well! I've got amazing things to tell you! But what about Stelios? He hasn't appeared yet...."

Kouvelas shrugged his shoulders.

"From what I know, he might not appear at all," he said. "Maybe it wasn't a good idea to drag him out too – he's only half a man.... In any case, you can see that we haven't done too badly."

He got into Lulu and was leaning over to open the passenger door for Minas, when his friend tapped on the window with his knuckle to attract his attention to something.

It was Marmaro, squeaking and groaning, who was coming into the square. Lulu flashed his lights and the deux chevaux came the wrong way round the square and stopped facing the sedan. It was quite clear that in the joy of having found his friends again and his utter exhaustion Lambrinos was past paying attention to the highway code and oblivious of the traffic signs saying No Entry.

Sweating, bright red, his hair on end, beating his arms against his thighs as he spoke – like he always did – Stelios was panting, tripping over his words and struggling to explain, to describe, to tell them all about his adventure that night. The only thing that Petros and Minas could understand at the beginning was that Stelios was outraged: something terrible had happened. Then they understood that the story was a long one and important and that the smallest detail of it was significant; and they began to be impatient. Kouvelas, like every time that he played truant from home, was now wanting to get back as soon as possible: it was a curious sense of balance that made him consider every minute spent away from Veronica wasted, when once the delight of the illicit had come to an end. Minas, too, was consumed with the desire to find Betsy again; the idea that she was waiting for him there in the garage, all alone, was haunting him.

Lambrinos, however, seemed prepared to keep them there all night to tell them about prohibited zones, about inhuman machines, interrogations, sergeants and military policemen, about a whole world which existed unsuspected alongside them, among them, about poisonous breaths, about compulsion, policing and countless other things.

One thing, though, stood out from among all this jumble of happenings – the man had left home perfectly fine, had taken Marmaro, and had done nothing less than end up at the radio station of the American base at Nea Pangri, which they all knew existed, and about which no one could understand why Stelios was making all this fuss, as if he hadn't known. It could have been worse. They looked at each other, and both knew what the other was thinking: "Something like this could only have happened to Lambrinos!"

"In case you're interested, Betsy has been found," Minas said to Stelios.

Their friend was dropping from exhaustion. It was obvious from the blank stare with which he greeted this news. They suggested that he should get a taxi to Batané and leave the deux chevaux here; they would pick it up tomorrow. Stelios hesitated.

"No, Minas," he said. "It doesn't matter any more – anyway I'm not in a hurry.... I'll go very slowly. I can't leave Marmaro here at night – it would be a sin...." (It was the first time they had heard him call the deux chevaux by her name.) "And since I'm half dead, I think I won't come down to Piraeus tomorrow. I need to rest. And I've got a few things to do...."

They said goodbye to him. It didn't matter if he didn't come to the office tomorrow. They would both be there to look after everything.

"Take care and don't go too fast!" said Minas, doubled up with laughter as they set off in Lulu, the two of them alone once more, to go to the Mobil station at Pashalimani.

"You were going to tell me something, if I remember right," Petros reminded him. "Amazing things that happened to you, you said...."

"Oh, yes," said Minas.

All his enthusiasm suddenly seemed to have evaporated.

"I met a girl," he said, and immediately blushed all over, his heart began to beat hard in his chest and an inexplicable feeling of hopelessness washed over him, as it had earlier in the evening. The lines of the poem again.... They came to his mind, like when he had learned about Betsy, when he had begun the search:

> *"Our two hearts will become great torches,*
> *their dual light reflect*
> *the twin mirrors of our minds."*

For the first time he did not find it easy to talk about a girl; for the first time he was filled with revulsion at the thought of recounting, describing, repeating and going over what had taken place, with Kouvelas or with anyone else. The details of their lovemaking, but also personal details about the girl, what she looked like, where she lived, her unexpected relationship to Betsy's thief – it all seemed like a treasure belonging to him alone, of which not an atom could be expressed outwardly – and specially not when served up in the crude language which they used when discussing such matters at the office. Till now his lovemakings had held no secrets from Petros – not even when it was with Evanthitsa. But about Gia....

And Petros did not seem in the mood to say very much about the funeral chamber.

"A wake" was all he said. "At the beginning I thought of pretending to be the doctor, just till I could find out if it was Soulis's house, but I changed my mind. I took on my coolest air, apologized for the misunderstanding and got out."

"And was it Soulis's house in the end?" asked Minas.

"Yes, it was," answered Petros. (Always tell whichever bits of the truth don't matter.)

"The bastard," thought Minas, "he's lying to me. So I don't have to reveal anything either."

At quarter past one, with Betsy leading and Lulu behind, they turned into the cool streets of Nea Kambara.

"Darling," Kouvelas said to Veronica, "here's Minas come to back me up."

Mrs. Kouvelas smiled, clearly relieved.

"Minas dear, I assume it's the perfect alibi," she said to Restis.

Minas smiled as well.

"All that remains is for me to use both of you to back me up tomorrow, so that I can face Eva," he said.

WITH THE NEXT MORNING'S DAWN CAME ANOTHER GOD-GIVEN summer day. While Miss Vipsy was making cold coffee for two in the shaker, with ice cubes, and Petros and Minas were preparing to receive Mr. Fokianos, Stelios woke late and went out to sit in the shade of the vine in the corner of the yard. He hadn't closed his eyes all night – only at dawn had he finally fallen asleep. His mother was sure that he was ill; one minute she asked him about his stomach, and the next about his digestion. With some trouble he warded her off.

"I'm just tired. There's nothing wrong with me...."

He leaned back against the whitewashed wall and, after examining his toes which were one metre seventy centimetres in front of him, he finally took off his glasses and placed them beside him. Now he could distinguish nothing except the light and the outlines of the door and the windows that looked onto the yard. And far off the hubbub of the square. He rummaged for his cigarettes, picked up Yellow Fellow, lit one. The first first few puffs of the first cigarette of the day always made him feel slightly dizzy. Then he got used to it.

There's nothing wrong with me, he said to himself as he remembered the old woman's bothersome ideas, now of calling the doctor, now of giving him some aspirin, now of making him a tisane. He had shouted at her and she left him in peace. Then he regretted it. Poor Mummy, she's the only person whom I can dominate, the only one who takes me completely seriously.

So he sat there and – God knows how or why – Stelios remembered school – that daily torment when you have to mix with a whole regiment of young cannibals who call you "squinty", "cross-eyes" or "blindman" or who put things on your seat so that you sit on them or who stick a bit of paper on your coat that says "Blind Eyes". And the only ally you have is the one person whom everyone else fears and loathes, the teacher. "Don't tease little Stelios, children! Aren't you ashamed of yourselves? Instead of giving him some support? Instead of helping him?" The teacher and I – one party – on the one hand. My fellow pupils (boys you would have liked to have as friends, girls you admired because they were beautiful) – another party – on the other hand. "But he doesn't want to be helped!" Dionysis told the class with the raw honesty of youth. And of course he didn't want to be helped! Their help was in itself a game at his expense; sooner or later children get bored with these roles. They hate sickly people and cripples because it's a contact with dissolution and death against which they rebel. Haroula pushed him away with both hands that day during break; her little face, crowned with her curly red mane, bore an expression of disgust and fear: "Leave me alone, cross-eyes!" He had come up to her in the shadow of the door by the little garden, ready to beg her, "Let me feel you up a little too...." which of course he didn't say but he was preparing to do it and if he had he didn't remember now. He felt something, he touched something; but what can you feel at that age except their little bums – for breasts they don't have. Haroula....

There's nothing wrong with me. A lifetime of pretending. Except that now I've just begun enjoying myself. Dr. Melis and the major wet themselves laughing. No, the machine had not broken down. It had simply given them unexpected results. Well, if you really want to know, I'm a type D person. D as in A,B,C,D. The machine categorized me as a cross between a pig and a goat. My intellectual parameters extend somewhere between my digestive tract and my genital system. Intelligence quotient – impossible to determine, because of the total inability to formulate concepts. This is what the Brain came up with. And as Dr. Melis says, the Brain doesn't make mistakes. And after they had laughed and passed the card round from hand to hand so that they could all admire the perfect formulation of the machine they unblindfolded me and untied me and wanted to offer me a coffee.... I told them to go to hell and said, "I am a lawyer and I shall protest to the authorities of my own country." And they didn't bat an eyelid, my friend. "Since you are a lawyer," the major said, "you will certainly know the appropriate steps to take." And I know perfectly well that they don't give a damn for us – either the authorities of my country or me. And why not? When it comes down to it I'm cross-eyed and instead of going to the Law Society to protest I might go to the cinema to see a morning porn film.

I wish I had read that bloody book of Christina's and knew it by heart – that one and all the others. If only my hate was theoretically well-grounded and my arguments scientific – as would befit the professional fellow that I am. If I could blow them all sky high! All those machines, all those rat traps.

Do you understand, my friend? You go out to help your pals and you fall into personality analysers, the Yankees truss you up in your own country and when they've reduced you to a rubbishy bundle of rags they throw you out without even saying they're sorry – neither them nor their fucking machines.

All my life I've been a Karaghiozis*.... And in truth neither of my friends has any need of me. They never have had. Tonight they managed fine by themselves. And instead of being open-mouthed at what I was telling them, they were in a hurry to get rid of me so that they could be alone and tell each other secrets and go to get

* Karaghiozis – the hunchbacked Greek popular shadow puppet: the little man pitted against life, surviving by his wits.

Betsy and celebrate, the two of them together, and talk about girls. And the odd man out, all on his own in the cold.... And there I was telling Petros and Minas about the terrible and disgusting things that happened to me, acting as if I wasn't ashamed of what I went through, to make them laugh so that they would like me – once again just like Karaghiozis. To amuse my Friends! Please excuse my Lateness! And my Handicap! Let them understand that, even though I ended up the devil's arse, I set out for them, to do them a favour. For Friendship. For Moral Support.... Never mind. So what? When I told them I wouldn't go in today – they didn't give a damn. Yes, stay at home and have a rest, he says, you need it. So they won't miss me. They've got other things, private things, to talk about today – I wasn't there, I wasn't playing with them, it's not my business at all.... But from today on I have other things to think of as well.... I've got to understand it. And when I understand I'll decide.... I just have to think, to manage to concentrate so that I can think precisely about the things that I have to – and nothing else!

There's nothing wrong with me. Nothing. I don't want tisanes or aspirin. Or an enema. What I want is one more fag. Oooops! Here's the fag.... Faggy-fagcanI-justlightyou?

"Click!" said Yellow Fellow.

"My friend," said Stelios, and he caressed him between his thumb and forefinger.

THE GANG WAS PLAYING TIG, THEIR SPECTATORS being the horses who had put their heads over the stable doors to watch and were whinnying, revealing their large yellow teeth. The sun was falling vertically on the grass through the leaves of the eucalyptus trees which, with each breath of breeze, were strewing the ground with their cone-like flowers.

Cosmas had stopped, deadbeat; his tongue hanging out, he was watching the others continue to play.

"Water, babe, water," he said, turning his head towards Mitsos who was lying on the ground with his eyes lazily half-closed.

"The tap's over there," he replied. "You've gone crazy running today in this heat."

"It's not the heat. It's yesterday's food. That man puts too much salt in it."

"Ha ha! It's the salt that bothers you, is it? So maybe you'd like to change restaurants?"

Cosmas understood his irony.

"After yesterday's episode I shouldn't think he'll bother us again," he said.

"That's what I think too.... But you never know. Cats are somewhat crazy animals."

When Cosmas got back from the tap his nose was wet. Mitsos, his eyes still half-closed, watched him curiously. Cosmas had shaken himself well, but funny little streams continued to run down the sides of his nose.

"Do you remember old Fondas?" Mitsos asked after a moment.

Cosmas looked at him.

"Come and have a run," he proposed.

Mitsos winked encouragingly.

"Come and lie down here," he said benevolently. "We'll have a run later. It's good to remember friends. That way they go on staying with you for a long time."

ALEXIS PANSELINOS

Alexis Panselinos was born into a literary family, in Athens, where he lives today. He is the son of Assimakis Panselinos, the poet, critic and author of a very popular autobiography. He studied Law at Athens University Law School and works as a lawyer. A very precocious writer, but a severe critic of his own writings, he only published his first book (*Dog Stories*, KEDROS, a collection of four short novels of which *Betsy Lost* is the third) in 1982, when he was nearing 40. This book won him immediate recognition as one of the leading contemporary Greek novelists. His first full-length novel, *The Great Procession* (KEDROS, 1985) won second state prize in 1986 and has been translated into French by Henri Tonnet (Editions Griot, Paris, 1995). *The Great Procession* was received with acclaim by both critics and the public and has already been reprinted six times. Then came his equally successful second novel, *Ballet Nights,* in 1991 (KEDROS) and shortly after this, in 1993, *Test Flight* (KEDROS), a volume of essays and articles on art, ideology and politics, mainly selected from among those previously published in important Athens literary reviews – though also including some appearing for the first time. He is currently writing his third big novel, eagerly awaited by the select public to whom he has become something of a "cult writer".

CAROLINE HARBOURI

Caroline Harbouri was born in London and educated at Cambridge University, where she studied English and French. Since 1970 she has made her home in Athens.

LIST OF TITLES IN THE "MODERN GREEK WRITERS" SERIES

PETROS ABATZOGLOU *What does Mrs. Freeman want*
Novel. Translated by Kay Cicellis

ARIS ALEXANDROU *Mission Box*
Novel. Translated by Robert Crist

SOTIRIS DIMITRIOU *Woof, Woof, Dear Lord*
Short Stories. Translated by Leo Marshall

MARO DOUKA *Fool's Gold*
Novel. Translated by Roderick Beaton

EUGENIA FAKINOU *Astradeni*
Novel. Translated by H. E. Criton

ANDREAS FRANGHIAS *The Courtyard*
Novel. Translated by Martin McKinsey

COSTIS GIMOSOULIS *Her Night on Red*
Novel. Translated by Philip Ramp

MARIOS HAKKAS *Kaisariani and the Elegant Toilet*
Short Stories. Translated by Amy Mims

GIORGOS HEIMONAS *The Builders*
Novel. Translated by Robert Crist

YORGOS IOANNOU *Good Friday Vigil*
Short Stories. Translated by Peter Mackridge and Jackie Willcox

IAKOVOS KAMBANELLIS *Mauthausen*
Chronicle. Translated by Gail Holst-Warhaft

ALEXANDROS KOTZIAS *Jaguar*
Novel. Translated by H.E. Criton

MENIS KOUMANDAREAS *Koula*
Novel. Translated by Kay Cicellis

MARGARITA LIBERAKI *Three Summers*
Novel. Translated by Karen Van Dyck

GIORGOS MANIOTIS *Two Thrillers*
Translated by Nicholas Kostis

CHRISTOFOROS MILIONIS *Kalamás and Achéron*
Short Stories. Translated by Marjorie Chambers

COSTOULA MITROPOULOU *The Old Curiosity Shop on Tsimiski Street*
Novel. Translated by Elly Petrides

KOSTAS MOURSELAS *Red Dyed Hair*
Novel. Translated by Fred A. Reed

ARISTOTELIS NIKOLAIDIS *Vanishing-point*
Novel. Translated by John Leatham

ALEXIS PANSELINOS *Betsy Lost*
Novel. Translated by Caroline Harbouri

SPYROS PLASKOVITIS *The Façade Lady of Corfu*
Novel. Translated by Amy Mims

VANGELIS RAPTOPOULOS *The Cicadas*
Novel. Translated by Fred A. Reed

YANNIS RITSOS *Iconostasis of Anonymous Saints*
Novel (?) Translated by Amy Mims

ARIS SFAKIANAKIS *The Emptiness Beyond*
Novel. Translated by Caroline Harbouri

DIDO SOTIRIOU *Farewell Anatolia*
Novel. Translated by Fred A. Reed

STRATIS TSIRKAS *Drifting Cities*
A Trilogy. Translated by Kay Cicellis

ALKI ZEI *Achilles' fiancée*
Novel. Translated by Gail Holst-Warhaft